Grave Warnings

Grave Warnings

A Short Story Horror Anthology

Edited by
Robert Mammone, Bob Furnell & Jez Strickley

Published by Pencil Tip Publishing
Vancouver, BC, Canada

www.penciltippublishing.com

First Published December 2016

ISBN: 978-0-9953195-0-9

Editors
Robert Mammone, Bob Furnell & Jez Strickley

Deceased Estate © Sarah Parry
The Dumb Show © Craig Charlesworth
The Specimen © Jodie van de Wetering
The Citizen © Hannah G. Parry
Vacancy © Hamish Crawford

Cover designed by Jack Drewell
Interior design by Bob Furnell

Typset in Times New Roman & Ghostwriter

The moral right of the authors has been asserted. All characters in this publication are fictitious and any resemblance to any persons living or dead is purely coincidental. All rights reserved. No part of this publication may be reproduced or transmitted in any forms by any means, electronic or mechanical including photocopying, recording or any other information retrieval system, without prior permission, in writing, from the publisher. This book is sold subject to the condition that it shall not, by way of trade or otherwise, be lent, resold, hired out, or otherwise circulated without the publisher's prior consent in any form of binding or cover other than that in which it is published and without a similar condition including this condition being imposed
on the subsequent purchaser.

CONTENTS

Deceased Estate by Sarah Parry	7
The Dumb Show by Craig Charlesworth	33
The Specimen by Jodie van de Wetering	65
The Citizen by Hannah G. Parry	73
Vacancy by Hamish Crawford	99
Author Biographies	125
About the Editors	127

Deceased Estate
Sarah Parry

I've never written one of these before. I don't suppose many people have, not unless they're serial killers or something, and I've never been one of those. I don't want anyone to think that I'm one of those either. I'm not here because of that, you have to believe me. It's just that I want protection, you see, and this seems the best way - the only way - of going about it.

* * * * *

I wasn't the one who purchased the house. It was Thwaites who had found it, and managed to wrangle it off the auctioneer for half its value. It wasn't the first property we'd bought up cheap – as long as you kept an eye out for deceased estates, you could get anything. And we needed more than anything, we needed a miracle. It wasn't that we hadn't made a name for ourselves in the property business, we had one of those. We were the guys that would sell you a house that was guaranteed to fall down within three days of your signing the papers for it. That was the problem with deceased estates – you got everything that the owners had left, all the chattels and furnishings and wallpaper, and also the dry rot, the mildew, and the cockroaches.

As I said, it wasn't the first house we'd bought up cheap, but we had definitely paid the least for it. As soon as we drove up, I could see why. It stood in the middle of a scrubby-looking field, half swamp and half furrows of dirt that would have looked like swamp if the earth hadn't been so dry and cracked. The house itself was a towering, three storey monstrosity, standing up straight like a stalactite in the middle of the wasteland. It was made of what looked like solid brick, but it was so covered in slimy green moss I could hardly make it out. The wind chose just that moment to send up a particularly fierce gust, rattling the bare branches of the birch tree next to the house and bringing with it the scent of mildew, and a dank, earthy smell that reminded me of the lions' cage at the circus.

"Well?" Thwaites said. "What do you think?" His broad face was scrunched into an expression of superior pride, and I had to stop myself from nodding on reflex.

"I think it's depressing as hell," I said. "It looks like a prison."

"You're a bigger idiot than I gave you credit for," Thwaites said dismissively. "Do you know who designed it?"

"Hannibal Lecter?"

"Freyberg," Thwaites sighed. "Franklin Freyberg? A little architect you might have heard of in one of those posh courses of yours?"

"You're kidding me." Of course I'd heard of him, long before I'd ever been to university. Freyberg had been something of a cause célèbre towards the middle of the nineteenth century, appearing on the design scene out of nowhere like he'd been hit with some sort of architectural divine inspiration. In this light, I turned back to look at the house before me.

"He must have been drunk," I decided.

"Well, they say this was the house he was working on when he died. Maybe he was senile."

"He was thirty-three when he died," I corrected. "He was found early one morning by his housemaid. The doctors said he died of overstretched nerves." I shook my head. "Are you sure this is one of his?"

"Positive. I've got the original plans right here," Thwaites pulled them from the back seat and threw them roughly into my lap. "Take a gander. I'll go and see if the keys work."

I looked at the plans barely long enough to convince myself that the elaborate signature scrawled on the bottom of the page was indeed Freyberg's, before hurrying after Thwaites.

He was still fumbling with the keys when I reached the front door, and I could see why. The lock was the largest and most elaborate thing I had ever seen. It seemed to have been cast from a solid piece of iron the size of my hand, with three separate keyholes drilled into it in a line.

"You need to do all three one after the other," Thwaites grunted, struggling with the final lock. "There's a trick to it..."

"Why?" I asked.

"Because that's the way your mad architect designed it, I suppose. The auctioneer explained it to me... There we go." The door swung open, groaning a little on its hinges. The strong, animal scent returned in force, almost assaulting me as it hit the back of my throat like a musty acid. I gagged, and Thwaites pushed past me into the entrance hall, looking around appraisingly.

"Not a lot in here to work with," he mused. "Let's try upstairs."

He disappeared up the stairs, and I leaned back against the wall, trying to get my bearings.

It was utterly dark. The thin, high windows let in almost no light, and absolutely no heat. The room I was in appeared to be empty - I could see a squat, misshapen lump in one corner that I hoped was a chair, and nothing else. For a moment, I just stood there and listened for the telltale creaks that all old houses have, especially when the wind was as fierce as it was that day. But all I could hear was the sound of Thwaites blundering around upstairs, and a muffled curse as he obviously nearly tripped over something in the dark.

It was then that I heard it. A scrabbling sound, like claws on rough wood, that made me look upwards. It was coming from inside the gap between the ceiling and the floorboards of the room above. It sounded like it was directly above my head.

Rats, I realized. Too big for mice, so it must be rats in the ceiling. Just what we needed.

I stood there in the mildew-damp darkness and listened to the sound come closer, skittering surely across the expanse –

probably running from Thwaites. But wasn't Thwaites heading across the floor from right to left, not left to right?

It stopped as suddenly as it had begun, and Thwaites came clattering back down the stairs. He was holding his lighter in one hand, and from the faint flame, I could see that his face was as sour as month-old milk.

"No lights," he said. "There might be a fuse box down in the basement, but I'm not risking my neck to find it in the dark. We've got some torches in the car, you can go get them." He kicked at the floorboards. "Still, it seems sound enough structurally. It could probably withstand a nuclear bomb. We'll be able to pass it off to some paranoid Doomsday-cultist. Or maybe some hippy will buy it as a rat sanctuary. From the sounds of things, we're overrun."

"You didn't see them?" I asked.

"No, they're under the floor. We'll lay some traps. I think I have a few in the car, you can have a look for them when you bring in the torches."

"Now? But I haven't looked over the house yet."

"Yeah, and you won't be able to do any looking if you don't fetch the ruddy torches, will you?" Thwaites made a move as if to hit me, then seemed to change his mind and sucked his teeth in derision. "Off you go – I'll see if I can start putting this place to rights."

* * * * *

I could have argued with him then, but I didn't. Truth be told, it was a relief to get out of that house, with its mildewed carpets and mould-slick walls. I couldn't believe Freyberg had designed it. I'd seen his work so often in textbooks, and I'd been to visit some of the houses he'd designed, cycling past them in my student days and dreaming of one day owning one, when I was rich. They'd always been grand, sweeping, pseudo-Italian affairs, like a Petrarchan love sonnet made of bricks and mortar. This place looked more like a dirty limerick. I couldn't imagine anyone being stupid enough to want to buy it.

The car was only parked a few paces away, but I took my time getting to it, and when I did I kept dawdling. I was sitting in the driver's seat with the door open, rooting aimlessly through the glove box for the torches when I heard the rattle of a bicycle wobbling by. I didn't bother to look up, but a few minutes later, when I realized it seemed to have stopped, I spared a glance in the direction of the road. Sure enough, there it was, leaning against the gate.

It was a nice bicycle, a Schwinn, and probably would have been worth a few bob eight or ten years ago, before the chains had rusted and the tires had lost their tread. Nowadays I doubted it would fetch you anything more than an incredulous stare at auction. The woman riding it got the same reaction from me.

"Can I help you?" I asked, hoping the answer was no. She was probably in her early fifties, and trying not to look it – all peroxide blonde hair and too much makeup. She gave me a smile that showed off the wrinkles around her eyes.

"You're the one that needs help love, if you're going in there," she said, looking behind me at the house. "They say it's a death trap."

"Well if it is, it's not working," I said. "There's enough rats in the place to warrant the second coming of the Pied Piper."

"Rats? Really? The place was always kept so neat in my time," the woman sighed. "Never saw so much as a sand fly in there when it was up and running."

"Well, there are now," I said. Although it didn't surprise me – her bright demeanour set my teeth on edge, I couldn't imagine what it would do to a poor insect.

"Mavis," the woman said, suddenly. I realized that it was her name at the exact same moment that I realized that it meant that she wanted the conversation to keep going. "May, people call me. Are you the new owners then?"

Ah. The local gossip mill in action, I thought. I probably shouldn't have mentioned the rats. I tried to think of something smooth and winning to say about the place, and failed. "Bought it this morning, apparently."

"You didn't know?"

"We'll not be living here," I said. "My partner and I buy up places, renovate them and sell them on. You'll be getting some new neighbours soon enough."

"You're renovating that?" she asked, nodding at the spectacle over my shoulder. "Good luck. Nobody's lived in it for close to ten years, not since Jim Freyberg and his wife died."

"Freyberg?" My ears, and my wallet, pricked up at that. "You mean the descendants of Franklin Freyberg, the architect?"

"Mm, that sounds about right. Jim used to say his grandfather designed the house. I used to do the cleaning here over the summer, back when it was up and running. It was a bed and breakfast, you know. Jim and Caro tried so hard to make it work – the house had been in their family for generations but it was beginning to fall apart and they needed the extra cash. The recession hit hard here." She sighed, brushing a strand of greying hair from her eyes. "Poor souls. They just couldn't make it work."

I looked back at the house, with its grim high windows and grime-caked timbers. "Well, I can see why they wouldn't have had too many takers."

"Oh, it didn't look anything like this back then," she assured me. "They painted it yellow, with white trim all around the windows. I didn't like it. It made it look a bit... odd. Like an armoured van trying to disguise itself as a tour bus. Still, people seemed to like it. They had a lot of guests – the prices were very cheap, especially for back then."

"I thought you said they needed the cash?" I frowned.

"They did – nobody could understand it. People kept telling them to raise the prices but they wouldn't. Didn't make much of a difference anyway, the amount of people who skipped out without paying."

"How did they manage that? The place has a lock the size of a Greyhound bus on the front door."

"Well, I don't know do I?" May sniffed. "But they usually did. Used to come by in the mornings to make the beds and find them all slept in, but the luggage was gone and their breakfast trays just sitting cold on the kitchen table. You just can't trust people any more, not these days, and not in those days either."

I nodded, but that didn't mean it made sense to me. "But why would they bother skipping out early if the prices were so cheap?"

"I've got a secret for you, love," May said. "People are awful. Remember that, and you'll go far."

"Yeah, I found that one out the hard way," I said dryly. I thought of Thwaites, stumbling and swearing around the house, and pulled the torches from the glove box. "I'd best be off – my friend may have been kidnapped by armed cockroaches or something."

"I'll let you get on with it then," May said. She pushed off from the wall, wobbling a little, and the bicycle began to sway its slow way towards the village.

* * * * *

Thwaites greeted me with a few choice swear words and lunged for the torches. "Where've you been?"

"Absorbing the local colour," I told him. "Apparently, this place used to be a B&B back in the day, except the guests never stayed around to pay for the privilege. According to my native guide, the place has been in the Freyberg family forever."

"Fascinating. You can put it in the brochure," Thwaites said. "If we can't sell the dump, we'll turn it into a museum and you can give tours."

I pulled a face, which he couldn't see in the darkness. He played the torchlight around the walls, taking in the blackened green wallpaper with disgust.

"We can probably wash it down and paint over the worst of the damage," I suggested. "And we can do the same to the rot in those windowsills. It's cheaper than re-wallpapering."

"Put your fine arts degree to good use," Thwaites agreed with a grin. "Do you want to check out the cellar? If you find the fuse box, give me a yell. I want to check out the rooms upstairs – some of the floorboards felt pretty shaky. If it's not too bad I'll just shove some carpeting over it.. Oh, the sale of the property included all the chattels inside it, by the way, so if you see anything valuable we can put up for auction."

"I'm on it," I said. He was already heading up the stairs, leaving me alone in the dark with the silence. I heard his footsteps retreating into the corridor, and saw the play of his torchlight, the slices of wallpaper and dusty furniture as the light caught them as he passed. Then I heard the faint stirrings of the rats in the ceiling above me again, and hurried towards the cellar.

The steps were rotting away, and I had to jump down the last three when they made an alarming noise – they'd probably have to be replaced, or we'd have to make sure the buyers never came down here until the place was sold. With a sigh, I turned my torch around the walls, searching for the fuse box.

The entire place was a mess, and it looked as though it hadn't seen the light of day since last century, if then. There were boxes, crates, old furniture, and so much other junk covered over with drop cloths that it was almost impossible to find a clear space to stand. There was enough rubbish to furnish another house. The animal smell was absent from here, but in its place was the stale scent of mildew. Water damage had stained the walls in filthy streaks, and formed glimmering black pools in the corners. Mounted in the midst of all of this sat the fuse box, covered in black slime.

I picked my way through the dusty old furniture, past the rocking horse with its rotting rope held tightly between its teeth, and pulled ineffectually at the door of the fuse box. All that happened was that I was left with my hands covered in sludge again. Grimacing, I put the torch between my teeth, and pulled at one of the drop cloths, intending to wipe my hands clean before I tried again.

What I saw then made me freeze. The blankets had concealed a pile of backpacks. There must have been close to twenty of them, all different colours and sizes, from small overnight bags to hiker's kits, with blankets strapped to the bases and saucepans on the front, faded and worn with time. Some of them still bore luggage tags: Harvey Dresser, from New York, Dana Field, who'd been to Uppsala, judging from the patches sewn to the back. Courtney Peach, Alex Coach, Peter Wakefield... the list went on, a list of backpacks with names firmly attached, suitcases still locked, possessions still held tightly inside.

I took a step back, feeling my mouth go dry. I tried to think of a rational explanation, and failed. The only thought I could cling to was that some of the non-paying backpackers had left their things behind, and the Freybergs had stored them down there, hoping they would come back to claim them. But hadn't May told me that they'd always taken their possessions with them? It made no sense. I didn't know what to think.

* * * * *

I don't know why I didn't tell Thwaites then and there, but I didn't. I suppose it was because I knew that really, what could I say? All Thwaites would have been interested in would be the value of whatever was in those bags, and on any other day, I would have been the same. But I didn't tell him. Maybe that makes everything that happened afterwards all my fault. I don't know. Maybe I could have stopped everything then and there, if only I'd had the will. But I didn't. Instead, I flipped the breakers, and headed back upstairs.

I'd like to say that the house looked entirely different in the light, but I didn't. All it did was make the shadows even more obvious.

I heard Thwaites give a whoop of satisfaction as I closed the door to the cellar, and a second later, he was clattering down the stairs. There was a strip of mouldering carpet that had probably once been red running right down the middle of the steps, and the banister rails were solid mahogany.

"Whole place is a death-trap," he said cheerfully. "Apart from that, it's as sound as a bomb shelter. Have you seen these walls?" He knocked on one of them, then winced. They sounded very solid. "Wood-panelled, quite tastefully, I might add. But I ran a drill through it – it's about a foot of what looks like solid brick in between us and the outer wall."

"I can't believe it still has running electricity," I said. I realized that my torch was still on, and turned it off. "I wonder who's paying the bill?"

"It's got a private generator," Thwaites sighed. "Honestly, why do you think I was talking about getting the lights on if it was on the national grid? They'd have cut off a derelict like this years back.. Unless you think the rats kept up with the bills?"

"I'm surprised they didn't chew through the wires. It sounds like there's enough of them to stage a bubonic plague convention."

"I'll call an exterminator tomorrow," Thwaites promised. "Did you find anything down in the cellar?"

"What, aside from the fuse box? Just a load of junk."

Thwaites wasn't listening. He had tilted his head back, looking around at the entry hall with almost a frown. "It's a bit of an odd design for a house, isn't it?" he said finally. "I mean, look at the locks on this door. Who would bother? I know you said the guests used to run out without paying, so it didn't seem to stop them legging it out a window."

"Have you seen the windows?" I asked. "You couldn't fit your arm out of one of those, they're far too narrow."

"The ones upstairs are no better – I couldn't even get them open. Who knows how the rats are getting in? Did you bring the traps in from the car?"

Of course I hadn't, he'd only asked for the torches. But it was getting late, and we were both impatient to leave, so I ran back to the car. It was beginning to rain, the encroaching clouds starting to fall in thick wet drops onto the windshield as I fumbled in the glove box.

By the time I made it back inside, I was wet, and Thwaites was all packed up. He sat in the car, blowing the horn as I struggled to tear the crust of my sandwiches into pieces small enough to fit into the traps. He stopped after a while, and I almost wished he hadn't. The irritating, muted foghorn noise made by the old pick-up was infinitely better than the silence of the rest of the house. It was so quiet it was almost like a noise in itself.

When the rats started up again, I was so shocked by the sudden sound that I dropped the mousetrap I was holding. It snapped against my hand like a crocodile, and I swore as a red line of blood sprung out across my thumb. The rats in the roof scrabbled faster, and a thin stream of dust fell from the ceiling and onto the floor, scattering among the mousetraps and across my outstretched arm. I glanced upwards, nervous. I found it all too easy to imagine the ceiling suddenly splintering, giving way under the weight of a thousand warm, hairy black bodies, covering me in a seething mass of claws and rabies.

When the car horn went again, I didn't hesitate. I left the mousetraps where they lay, haphazard in the dust, and ran, making sure I shut the front door firmly behind me.

* * * * *

It was still raining the next day, and I slouched to the house behind Thwaites with admittedly bad grace. It looked even worse than it had the day before.

There was a battered old pest control van parked outside that morning, which I noticed first. The second thing I saw was the battered old pest controller who drove it. Peters looked as if he'd been waiting for a while, judging by the cigarette butts lying outside his van, but his cheerful, garden-gnome face showed no sign of being annoyed. It only made me scowl a little harder. Peters had been in the business for as long as we had, and he'd known Thwaites for even longer. I didn't know how they'd met, but he charged next to nothing, and knew better than to ask too many questions. But he had a way of looking at you that made you feel that he was very aware of what he wasn't asking, and that always had a way of setting my teeth on edge.

"Lovely day for it," he said, hopping out of the van and following us into the house.

"If you're a duck," Thwaites snorted. "Still, at least this place doesn't leak. You brought your box of tricks with you?"

Peters nodded, and patted his backpack knowingly. "All in here. So, what are we dealing with? Rats, cockroaches? Both?"

"Probably," I said. "But we're mostly worried about the rats."

"They're up in the ceiling there," Thwaites explained. "I could hear the ruddy things following me about all day yesterday. Think you can take care of them?"

Peters beamed. "I should think so," he said. "Rather a lot of them, you think?"

"Does it matter?" Thwaites asked. "It's not as if you charge by the head."

"I wish I did. You know, I found a rat with two heads once. It was in an old house out by Fullerton, it was a deceased estate as well. You find the oddest things in places like this." He looked around him at the mouldering entrance hall. "Very odd."

"Right. Well, we'll leave you to it, then," I said. "I've got work to do in the cellar." I didn't really, but I knew from experience that I didn't want to hang around to hear Peters' running commentary on the delicate art of mass rodenticide.

"I'll be up on the roof," Thwaites added. "If you find anything down in the cellar you want burnt, let me know. We'll have a bonfire and get rid of some of the junk."

I nodded, and made a quick exit downstairs. I hadn't been looking forward to the idea of going back down there, but I'd given myself a stern talking to last night. There were a hundred reasons why there might be a stack of backpacks left lying around – guests might have forgotten about them, or they might have belonged to the Freybergs. They might have collected them. Whatever the reason, it wasn't worth worrying about. The Freybergs were dead, and that was the end of it. I didn't even bother taking the drop cloths from them – I just scooped up the whole lot and threw it in a pile in the corner to be burnt. It fell against the concrete with a clatter of pots and pans, and the sound was oddly satisfying. I turned my back on them, and got to work.

Most of the books were fairly commonplace – a few Reader's Digest classic hardbacks, a stack of old womens' magazines and a few scattered paperbacks with impossibly romantic covers. I threw them all on the 'burn' pile and moved on to the furniture. It was all old, heavy dark wood pieces that nobody wanted to buy anymore. My contact at the auction house would probably make me pay him to take them off my hands. I was going through the drawers out of a lack of anything else to do when I heard something rattling around in the bottom drawer of an old dresser. It was the same dark wood as the rest of the furniture, but the mirror had smashed at some point, and this drawer, unlike the others, was locked.

It was the matter of a moment to force it open with an old chisel, and pull out what was inside.

It was heavy, and wrapped in a thick piece of black cloth, which I pulled off to reveal an old, metal-clasped book. The black leather of the cover was cracked, but unmarked – it had no title, and even when I checked the spine and pulled open the clasp to check the front page, there was nothing. It was too heavy to hold upright, so I set it down on top of the dresser, and opened it up properly.

At first, I was a little disappointed. I had hoped for a diary – the lost, secret thoughts of Franklin Freyberg. Maybe it would have told us something about the house, like just what he'd been smoking at the time of its conception. But it wasn't a diary. I didn't know what it was.

It was written in Latin, and it looked like it had been done by hand. The pages were as thin as a butterfly's wings, and I was terrified I would tear them. I knew that I should simply close it again, and keep looking through the rest of the items in the cellar, but somehow I couldn't put it down.

I can't remember most of what I saw in that book. I remember that there were pictures, and I remember staring for what felt like a year and half at the image of a beautiful woman standing before a mirror, with a skeleton for a reflection. There was another of a man with what looked like eyes in the back of his head, but they weren't like any eyes I had ever seen before. I turned over that page before I had the chance to look at it too closely in case I recognized them.

I was about halfway through when I opened to a page and a bookmark fell out. I stared at it, where it laid on the floor for a moment, and then turned to the pages it was marking.

To this day, I wish that I hadn't. I'll never forget what I saw.

Some of the Latin words on the first page were underlined, quite firmly, as if the author wanted to make something very clear, but it was gobbledygook to me. What wasn't, or at least, what was slightly clearer to me, was the picture it was describing.

There was a man sitting on the floor, surrounded by piles of coins and precious stones. The picture was only black ink, but I could almost see the blood-red gleam of the rubies, and the gold glinting like a sunrise. The man was smiling, and I found myself smiling back, although I didn't know why. There was something about his face, the look of contentment in his eye, of satisfaction.

Then I looked again, and I saw that his smile was only the smile of a skull.

It was a corpse. Content, languid, sitting – no, *held* upright by the pile of wealth scattered around it. And stretching out among the gold like branches, were bones. Scraped bare of flesh, but still recognizably human. I almost didn't notice what was behind it, but when I did, I didn't realize how I could have missed it.

It looked like it could almost be human. Bent double on all fours, like an old man or a beggar searching for crumbs on the ground, its emaciated frame hung with the tattered remains of clothes, or flesh – I couldn't tell. It had teeth, each one wickedly curved like the fangs of a snake, and it was crawling through the gold like a fly over refuse. One spindly, long-nailed hand was curled over the arm of the corpse.

The worst part was, somehow, I felt as if I had seen it somewhere before.

I closed the book with an effort, and simply stared at the cover. My hands shook, and like I was going to be sick.

The book was heavy in my hands, and I could feel my sweat slicking the cover. Without even thinking, I threw it on the junk pile.

* * * * *

I came back up from the cellar nearly an hour later, feeling a lot calmer. The book had scared me, of course it had – the pictures in it were enough to give anybody a case of the creeps. But it was just a book, and now it was on its way to becoming so much ash. Part of me was beginning to regret putting it on the pile. It looked ancient, it was probably very valuable. I'd even come up with a theory about it – maybe it was one of those moral lesson books, trying to scare people away from sinful behaviour. One of the words on that page that was underlined had sparked a memory somewhere, of a Latin course that I had failed. "Vorax". Meaning 'hungry'. Maybe it had been a warning about greed? Don't be greedy or... you'll turn into a skeleton? Starve to death? The thing crawling through the gold had certainly looked hungry enough.

I was still thinking those thoughts as I locked the cellar door behind me, and nearly banged directly into Peters. His cheerful expression had dimmed a little, his broad face drawn into a look of puzzlement.

"Oh, sorry," he said. "Didn't see you there." He gave me one of his nervous, beaming smiles.

I nodded, and turned to go.

"It's just –" Peters caught me by the arm, stilling me. "It's just... well, it's the rats."

"Lots of them were there?" I said casually. "Did they have two heads?"

"No, well, I suppose I shouldn't have said 'the rats'. I mean, the problem is related to them–"

"Peters."

"There weren't any."

I stared at him. I felt myself grow cold, as if someone had just opened a window to the cold, grey rain outside. "What?"

"That's exactly what I thought," Peters said, some of the enthusiasm creeping back into his voice. "I mean, Thwaites did say that there were rats, didn't he? He said he heard them-"

"Under the floorboards upstairs, yeah," I said. "I heard them too. It was hard not to hear them, the place must be overrun."

Peters shook his head. "There's not a one," he said. "I found some remains of rats, but they're very old. Here, have a look?"

"No, that's fine, I-"

But Peters was already pulling something out of his pocket, and as soon as I saw it, I couldn't look away. A tiny rodent skull, as white as only bone can be. There was something quite pathetic about it, with its blank, empty eyes staring up at the ceiling and it's too-sharp teeth fixed in a permanent, fleshless smile.

"Very nice," I said uneasily.

"I collect them," Peters explained. "There's a bit of damage, some teeth marks around the orbits there," he ran the edge of a finger around the tiny eye sockets, and I could see what he'd meant. "Poor thing must have been gobbled up by his mates." He popped it back into one of the big, zip-up pockets of his overalls, and patted it securely. "Apart from that, it's been a very disappointing day. Not a pest to be had for neither love nor looking."

"There must be – maybe they heard you coming and hid."

"In this house?" Peters shook his head. "I've been over every inch of it; it's solid as a rock. Not so much as a gap in the plasterwork, for all its dilapidation. Not even air could get in or out of here once the windows were closed and the door locked, I'd wager."

"But that doesn't make any sense. What was making that noise, then? Cockroaches? Spiders having a dance party?" I crossed my arms and looked at him, challenging.

"No spiders, no cockroaches either," Peters said. "Fascinating really. Must be something in the wood acting as a natural pesticide, that's all I can guess. I haven't seen so much as a dust mite in here."

"That can't be-" But it was true, I knew it even as I started speaking, and the words died, stillborn on my tongue. I'd seen mould, and plenty of it. But I hadn't seen any cobwebs. Not even in the cellar, among those old boxes and books.

"You must have just heard the floorboards creaking," Peters was saying, and I tried to focus back on his voice. "The house settling, or whatever it is you call it. You two have been around enough old death traps like this one to know how it can play tricks on you."

"What did you say?" My voice must have sounded panicked, or at least strained, because Peters' face frowned even more as he looked at me.

"It must have been the house settling," he repeated slowly. "You know, when the weather turns warm, and the floorboards and such expand in the heat-"

"No, not that," I said. "Afterwards. What did you call the house?"

"Oh..." Peters frowned. "A death trap?"

"Yes," I said. "Why did you call it that?"

He looked flummoxed for a second. "Well, it's a common enough phrase, isn't it?"

"Yes," I said. "Sorry, yeah, it is. It's just, you're the third person to call it that."

"There you are, then. It is a common phrase." Peters shook his head. "Come outside for a bit. The rain will clear your head. You've been down in that dusty cellar all morning. You can walk me to my car, I've got a thermos of tea in there, we can have a brew and-"

"I'm fine," I said. "Really, yeah, I'm fine. It's just... you're right, I've been down in that cellar too long." I cleared my throat, and managed a passable smile, the sort I usually give to clients when they ask if I know if a property has a history of water damage. "I'll just... Thwaites is outside, up on the roof. Give him a shout and he'll come down and settle your fee. Sorry for wasting your time."

It was a few more minutes before I was able to get rid of him, but as soon as I had, I went straight back to the main hall, and checked the mousetraps I had laid the night before.

They were exactly as I had left them, empty, the crust from my sandwich still un-nibbled. And it would be, if there weren't any rats in the house.

I sighed, not sure what I had been looking for in the first place. There were no rats. It was a good thing. For once, I'd be able to sell a house that had no history of pest problems. We could claim we'd had a licensed pest controller through, and he hadn't been able to find a thing to justify his fee. A deceased estate without a single sign of life.

It was only when I turned to leave that I remembered the blood I'd left on the floor the night before, when my fingers had caught on one of the springs. I pulled a tissue out of my pocket, ready to wipe it up.

But there wasn't anything to clean. I checked around both mousetraps, looking for the telltale smudge of rust-coloured stain, but there was nothing there.

My heart stilled a little. Thwaites must have come in and done it this morning. Maybe it had soaked into the wood, or evaporated. Maybe it hadn't been as much as I had thought.

I thought of the rat skull, with the thick, angry gouges around its eyes, and I almost ran from the room.

* * * * *

I didn't go back down to the cellar after that. I didn't go anywhere. I sat in the old, faded chair in the entranceway and tried not to think about all the strange things in the house. There was no point. We would be selling it soon enough. Thwaites was confident we could have it back on the market by the end of the week. At one point, I pulled out my phone and looked Freyberg up on the internet, but there was nothing there that I didn't remember from my courses. He had had a short but brilliant career, and died obscenely wealthy and of unknown causes. The only fact that I didn't remember was that just before his career had kicked off, his wife, the mother of his children, had walked out on him in the middle of the night. Despite the concerted efforts of half the constabulary in England, it seemed, she had never been seen again. The common theory was that all of his work had somehow been inspired by his heartbreak.

I thought of the backpacks lying in a pile at the bottom of the house, and made myself turn off the phone.

It was nearly nightfall by the time Thwaites came back in, and the rain had started to let up. He'd been up on the roof for most of the day, and in an even fouler mood than usual, especially when he saw me lounging in the chair scrolling through my phone.

"I'll burn that junk of yours downstairs tomorrow when we cart the rest out to the auction house," Thwaites sighed, after he'd thoroughly chewed me out. I don't remember exactly what he said to me, although now I wish I did. "Anything worth much?"

"Not really. The value of the place is in the name of the designer."

"Glad to hear it. Otherwise, the property's not even worth what we paid for it. Who'd want to live here?" He gestured around the room disdainfully. "And it *smells*. We should get going."

"Mm. In a minute. I left something in the cellar."

I don't know why I said that. Maybe it was because the image of that picture in the book had been burning in my brain all day, but I had to look at it again. If only to prove to myself that it wasn't what I had thought it was. It wasn't as scary, or as... I didn't know what, but I had to see it and know.

"Well, hurry it up, then." Thwaites crossed his arms, leaning back against the wall. "We don't have all night."

The book was where I had left it, lying in the corner, half under a pile of junk. It was a matter of moments before I had it, and ran back up the stairs.

"What's that, then?" Thwaites asked, curious.

"A book."

"Yeah, I can see that. Valuable?"

"Probably not. Shall we go?"

He was about to say yes, but the sound of the door slamming shut cut off how he'd planned to say it. We both turned to look at it.

"Well, that sounds like our cue to leave," Thwaites said cheerfully. He tugged on the handle, then frowned. "It's locked," he said.

"Don't play games," I sighed. "Just open the door."

He fumbled for the key in his pocket. "I will in a minute, but it's..." he frowned, staring at the door handle. "There's no keyhole," he said.

There wasn't. The doorknob, huge and elaborate as it was, had no place for a key. Thwaites rattled the handle, then I did. It was definitely locked.

"Who designs a door with a lock only on one side?" Thwaites growled. "What sort of genius architect? For that matter, what sort of genius architect designs a door that locks on its own? I certainly didn't do it. Did you?"

"How could I? I've been inside all day, and as we've just discovered, the door only locks from the outside! I-"

I stopped, and stared up at the ceiling. A fine layer of dust was falling to the floor, catching and glittering in the moonlight. A moment later, and I heard the slow, languid scratch of claws on wood.

"I'm going to bloody kill Peters," Thwaites sighed. "He charges fifty quid for a call-out fee, and claims he can't find anything to waste his precious chemicals on? I'll have him."

The scratching was getting louder, and suddenly, it wasn't in the floorboards any more. The echo changed, subtly, and I don't know why but I knew it was quite clearly above us. Standing in the room directly over our heads.

I thought of the creature in the book that I had seen, with its nails like claws, and its wicked teeth. I thought of them scraping against bone, against wood and tearing flesh and fabric and floorboards like paper.

"Let's get out of here," I said quickly. I pulled my phone out of my pocket. I'd been using it a lot today, but there was still quite a bit of battery left. "I'll call the police, or the fire brigade or something – they'll let us out."

"Yeah, and charge the earth for it," Thwaites snorted. "I've got a property valour coming in first thing, we can just bed down here for the night."

I had already made the call. "Hello? Yes, it's an emergency. My friend and I, we're stuck in the old Freyberg house just outside Millview. Can you send someone, please? Quick as you can, this place is-"

Thwaites pulled the phone out of my hand, and cut the call. "What are you doing? Are you insane?"

"We're not breaking the law!" I argued. "It's our house we're stuck in; we have the right to ask the police for help!"

"Yeah? And if they catch sight of some of the dodgy building practices we've gotten up to, what's stopping them from hauling us both down the station for a longer talking to? They know I've got form, I've already lost my builder's registration. I'm using polystyrene to block up the gaps in the garage roof, for crying out loud!"

I was clutching the book tightly to my chest, and I could almost feel my heart hammering against it. The covers were clammy, and it was as heavy and solid as a brick pressing down against me. I could barely breathe against the crush, but I could not lighten my grip.

"Thwaites," I said slowly. "There is something about this house that I don't like. I've never liked it, and I especially don't like it now that I'm trapped inside of it. There's too many strange... things. Disappearing lodgers and books, and... We need to get out of here." Away from the rats, I thought. Please, let us get away from the rats, because there aren't any rats in this house, so what is making that *noise*?

"We will, in the morning," Thwaites said, with exaggerated patience. "Look, I'll even let you have the chair. I'll sleep upstairs; I think there's a bedroom somewhere–"

"Don't go upstairs! That's where the rats are!" The words flew out of my mouth before I could catch them, panicked and desperate.

"I'm not scared of a few rats." He was getting annoyed now. Even with only the light from the moon, I could see his expression in my mind's eye. "I always knew you were squeamish, but this is something else. Now, I'm going upstairs, and I'm going to scare those rats of yours back into hiding. If you dare to call the police again, I'll have your hide when I get back downstairs, do you understand me?"

"Thwaites–"

"Stay. There." He turned to go up the stairs. For a second I caught the flash of his expression in the moonlight, disgusted, imperious, and then he was gone.

* * * * *

I should have followed him. I would like to write that I did, because if I could go back and do it again then I would. But I didn't. I stayed where I was, still holding onto that book; while I heard Thwaites mount the stairs. He was hurrying up them, angry, determined, and I was shaking so hard that it almost hurt. The stairs creaked, and the sound of his step grew fainter and fainter.

The rats had stopped. I couldn't hear anything from them. I could barely hear anything over the clamour of my racing heart, and my breath in my ears. It almost hurt to breathe. The scent of the house, the mildewed, animal smell was back, stronger than before. I wanted to run, I could feel the adrenaline burning in my legs, but there was nowhere to run to. I was trapped.

Thwaites was making his way across the floor now. I could hear the dull thud of his footsteps, his muffled curses as he struggled to find the light switch, and the growl when he failed. He must have turned his torch on then, because he stopped still, and I heard nothing more.

I can see him now, playing the thin beam around the room, sending it into the corners, dancing it across the walls, seeing only the mildewed wallpaper, the broken furnishings. No sign of any rats.

And then I heard him scream.

There was a scrabbling of claws like rain on a windshield, and Thwaites kept screaming. I must have screamed as well – my throat felt awful afterwards, but I don't remember. I just remember racing up those stairs so quickly I thought my heart would explode from my chest.

It was easy to see where he had gone – the light from his torch was shining through the darkness, swinging wildly as it rolled across the floor, still reeling with the momentum of its sudden fall. I caught myself in the doorway, frozen, stiff with fear.

I didn't see Thwaites' body, not at first. It was lying there, with its back broken and lines of blood across its face. What remained of his face, anyway. He didn't look anything like a human being any more, it was just meat, and the white glint of bone in the moonlight. It was the sort of thing you couldn't not look at.

Unless there was something worse to see.

It was crouched over Thwaites with its back to me, but the moment I came in to the room, it turned and fixed me with its gaze instead.

You know what it looks like. I showed you the book, you took it off me. I'll never forget it. It was white, like bone, or something that had never seen the sun. Except where it was covered in Thwaites' blood. But the worst part was its eyes. They were famished, open and staring, and as yellow as jaundice. Its claws were out, resting against the floor, and I could see blood on them, and on the floor.

I didn't scream then. I didn't make a sound. I just stood there, staring at it. Unable to move, unwilling to think. It was going to kill me. The way it had killed Thwaites. The way it had killed all of those lodgers. The way it had killed Freyberg's wife.

I knew what it was, then. I knew what the book had been trying to warn against. The book could make you rich and famous, if that was what you wanted, but there would have to be a cost. Greed for greed, this creature would match you, follow you, and take in blood whatever you took in wealth. I don't know where Freyberg had found it, or what had possessed him to use it, but he had. And everyone had paid the price for it. Freyberg's wife had been the first. She had never left him, never disappeared. I don't know if he knew when he found the book that she would be the first to pay for his success, but he knew someone would be.

But there must have been a time limit – Freyberg's heart had given out, his nerves had failed, at the end of a ten year career. The creature hadn't killed him, but he must have known he was dying, no matter how shocked everyone else had been. That was why he had built the house for it. A perfect cage, with his grandchildren keeping it fed, offering up victims to it that could be explained away whenever they disappeared. They had tried to keep it going, maybe hoping it would work the same miracle for them as it had for their grandfather. It hadn't. They had died poor. Whatever spell was in the book I held, it didn't work for just anyone. Nobody could control it any more.

Then the creature's eyes locked with mine, and it *smiled*.

* * * * *

That's when you came in. You broke the door down, and it was gone. I didn't see it leave. I couldn't look at it, I didn't like the way it was looking at me, and I had to look away.

Maybe it was because of the book. I want to think it was because of the book, and not because of me. Not something I did, or didn't do. Not because I didn't tell Thwaites about the book, or because I went back for it. I don't want to think that I wanted any of this. Freyberg had ten years. I'll only be forty. Forty's too young, isn't it?

You did lock the door behind you, didn't you? When you broke it down, did you fix it up afterwards, so that the lock works? It's very important, that lock. It held it for a hundred years, it has to keep holding it. Did you fix the door? Did you check the lock?

*****

"Is this the last of them?" DC Chesterfield asked, nodding at the neatly typed and printed transcript. It was getting late. He wanted to get home.

The officer behind the desk nodded, fingering the top of the file nervously.

"Yeah. Pretty tragic case, that last one. Have you read it? The poor bloke we pulled out of that house last night. The one where we found Harold Thwaites."

"Thwaites? The one with the..." Chesterfield ran his hand across his face, the fingers curved like claws.

"Yeah, that's the one."

"And his mate's in custody?"

The desk sergeant nodded. *"What's left of him. They say his mind's gone. They've got him in a holding cell, can't get him to leave."*

"What are they going to do with him?" Chesterfield frowned, flicking absently through the statement.

"He'll get sectioned off to the funny farm. Keep him in a nice cell with white walls."

Chesterfield nodded. *"Right,"* he said, adding the folder to the pile. *"Tragic."*

A sudden noise caught his attention, and he looked upwards automatically. A short, sharp sound, like claws on metal, ran swiftly across the ceiling, away from the desk, and in the direction of the cells beyond.

Chesterfield snorted. "Rats in the ceiling," he muttered. "Blasted pests."

The Dumb Show
Craig Charlesworth

It was a winter's day in London as fair and bright as any in the canon of Mr. Dickens - the sun hung brightly above, the ground beneath white and crisp and a snap of cold lingered in the air like a promise. Christmas, though, had lately passed from the calendar and New Year too had been and gone. The poor of the city in one of its less well-to-do districts went about their business looking rather forlorn for the knowledge that the festive season was past yet the cold and the snow remained. It was thus every winter, but this year was the first that Mr. Samuel Preston had been abroad in these parts of the city.

Mr. Preston, you see, was a man who had made out reasonably well in life. He had attained a degree in Law from a reputable school, and successfully parlayed this into a job with a small but reasonably successful London firm. On the death of his parents some years earlier he had been the sole beneficiary of their substantial estate, his younger brother Timothy being something of a disappointment to the family after running away at 16 to go to sea. Unlike his brother Samuel Preston was not the kind of man who ever acted rashly or impulsively, and therefore was very much the favourite of his father, a man who lived his life by the maxim that *"Spontaneity is the well from which bad sense drinks"*. He had made Samuel learn the phrase as a child, and would rap his son smartly across the knuckles with a ruler if he were unable to repeat it on command. And so, you can see plainly that between his large inheritance and his in-no-way mean salary, Mr. Samuel Preston was a man upon whom fortune had chosen to smile.

And why should it not be so? He was a kind and jovial man, who gave freely to charity and was not inclined to ill-use his wife, who loved him as much as he loved her. That is important in what is to come - let us not forget that Mr. Samuel Preston is no Ebenezer Scrooge. Neither you nor I must judge him too harshly for his later actions, for which he paid a hefty cost.

* * * * *

And now we are but a few lines into the tale and I have digressed already. We left Mr. Preston in one of the poorer districts of London, if I recall, though we had not discussed the reasons for his being there. You see, for all Mr. Preston's outward appearance of being a steady, trustworthy man of fine moral character and an appallingly boring nature, he did allow himself to indulge in one vice - the wagering of large sums of money on the outcome of horse races. Like most such men, he reckoned himself an expert in the subject without actually being anything of the sort, and so he had found himself - with alarming rapidity - divested of his house, his fortune and (by and by) his reputation. The next thing to go, alas, was his wife. And so, in his newly reduced financial circumstances, Mr. Preston had recently come into the market for affordable accommodation suitable for a single man, and no rooms in the city were cheaper than the ones of this particular district. Thus, he found himself, in that faintly depressing time just after the festive season but long before the spring, treading these benighted streets in search of the offices of one Mr. Moorcock, a landlord whom he had arranged to meet.

* * * * *

Mr. Moorcock conducted his business on the second floor of a ramshackle old building, his office occupying a single room which containing nothing more than a desk, a chair and a bookcase stuffed with ancient, dusty notebooks. Mr. Moorcock, too, seemed covered in a thin layer of dust, almost as if he sat inanimate in this room until such a time as his services were called on. Indeed, when

Mr. Preston entered the room he had to cough several times rather loudly before the old man awoke with a jolt, like some automaton that had been turned on suddenly and unexpectedly. Mr. Moorcock was of indeterminate age - he could have been anywhere between a hundred and several hundred years old, with his slightly yellowed hair curling down over a drawn and somewhat vacant face lined with fine wrinkles. On seeing his guest, he stood stiffly to attention and shook Mr. Preston's hand limply as the lawyer introduced himself.

"Well," said Mr. Preston after a few moments of silence. "I understand that you have some rooms to show me?" Mr. Moorcock shrugged, barely perceptibly and picked up a thin, worn out coat from the back of his chair. Then, with a sigh, the old man took a key from a small pile in his desk drawer and signaled for Mr. Preston to follow him.

* * * * *

The rooms were only a few streets away, but all manner of human villainy and moral decay littered those alleyways. Mr. Preston, for so long used to the rather more genteel side of London life, found himself, to his dismay, stepping over the prone forms of a number of men and women, most of them clutching half-empty bottles of cheap gin with all their remaining strength. All rich men are aware of the abstract concept of poverty, but few ever earn the opportunity to see it at such close quarters; Mr. Preston himself preferred dealing with the poor remotely - he gave to a number of charitable organisations, and he had rather hoped that this was as far as his contact would extend. Closer examination did little to change his mind on that point.

His mood improved, however, when he saw the rooms that Mr. Moorcock was renting. The building was squalid and dirty from the outside, its brickwork shoddy and the paint on the wooden doorframe peeling and chipped, but inside it was homely and almost pleasant. The rooms he was being shown were on the second floor and consisted of a decently sized living room with a rather grand fireplace and a good solid wooden floor, as well as a cozy and attractively furnished kitchen and a bedroom of a decent size. His initial pleasure, alas, was mixed with disappointment.

Surely these could not be the rooms that were being offered at such an astonishingly reasonable fee as Mr. Moorcock's advertisement had claimed?

"Tell me," said Mr. Preston when he had had a good nose around and satisfied himself that there must have been some mistake. "These are the rooms I enquired about when I contacted you? Forgive me if I seem a trifle curious but, and you'll think this an awful negotiating tactic, you could surely get double the money that you are asking?" Mr. Moorcock simply shrugged. These, he said in his monotone voice, were the rooms, and the price was the price. Now did Mr. Preston want them or not?

Of course, the answer was that he did, and he almost tore off his new landlord's hand in his indecent haste to shake on the agreement. Would that he had not.

*****

One week later, with the arrangements made, Mr. Preston moved into the little rooms. Despite his reduced circumstances he remained cheerful - these were the worst of times, to be sure, but he was confident that he would soon be financially stable once again and that once that feat had been achieved his wife would come back soon enough. Then all would be as right as nine pence, and life could go on much as it had done before the recent unpleasantness.

That first night, Mr. Preston lit a fire in the old fireplace and dined on a plate of bread and cheese with some slices of apple, all washed down with the best bottle of wine he could afford. Thus sated, he took his place in the little armchair that had come with the rooms, an ancient thing with faded green upholstery which may well have been fashionable a decade previously, and decided to read a few chapters before he made his way to bed. But the book was dull and the room warm, and soon enough he fell into a deep slumber. Several times he awoke with a start and began to think about going to bed, but the chair was comfortable and the fire cheery, and the thought of leaving either seemed as difficult as swimming the length of the Thames. And so, there he remained, until at last the book fell from his hands into his lap and he slipped into a deep, rather satisfied, sleep.

The clock of the church two streets away could be softly heard chiming the third hour of the morning when Mr. Preston awoke in a state of some agitation. He had been troubled by a dream, the details of which now seemed frustratingly vague as though the whole thing had been seen through some veil or miasma. He remembered being frightened; felt as though something was chasing him, and he found his heart thumped in his chest and his forehead was clammy with sweat.

This did not unduly perturb our hero for, despite his optimistic disposition, he had endured much anxiety of late over his gambling debts (which the sale of his house and all his worldly goods had not entirely managed to cover) and it was not unusual for him to allow, in his weaker moments, his mind to wander in the direction of shadows and horrors. He looked and saw that the fire had dimmed. The cold seeped in through the windows like a creeping, invisible fog and he pulled his clothes closer about him and shivered. And then, as he was just about to head finally toward his bed, something happened, something which would forever after alter his fate in ways he could not have foreseen. I shall try here to relate it as well as I am able, though I am afraid, that to grasp the full horror of it one really had to be there.

It began with the sound of a key rattling in a lock, except that this sound did not come from the door. Rather it seemed to come from everywhere at once - every corner of the room filled with a furtive metallic rustle as if some tiny mechanical bird had made its nest in the rafters and were flapping its wings to the beat of a funeral dirge. Now it must be noted that at this point that Mr. Preston, stout fellow that he was, was more annoyed than afraid at this. He did not know the source of this strange sound but he reckoned he knew one thing - that this must, surely, be the reason why the rent on these rooms was so unusually reasonable.

Presumably the noise was caused by something amiss within the structure of the building and Mr. Moorcock, too lazy to have the matter dealt with, had instead chosen to reduce the price of the rooms so as to attract a tenant so undiscerning that they would not make a fuss of being awoken at this indecent hour. Well, if Mr. Moorcock thought that of Samuel Preston he would have a rude awakening! Indeed, Mr. Preston was already planning in his mind a particularly strongly worded letter of complaint when he realised that the sound had stopped as suddenly as it had started.

With a shrug, Mr. Preston picked up his book from where it had fallen and prepared once again to go to bed. An investigation into the cause of the sound could wait until morning, and he was so damnably cold. Even by the standards of London deep in winter, he was positively freezing - the kind of cold that bites down on the marrow of your bones and bites hard: insatiable and merciless. Mr. Preston was just thinking that he should build his fire all the more fiercely the next night when he felt the hairs on his arms rise and a light electric shiver run along his spine. No, he thought: it wasn't the cold. It felt like the cold, but on some instinctive, animal level he was acutely aware that there was something else. Something worse.

Then there was a rustle of skirts and the sound of a lady laughing, high and clear. Poor Mr. Preston whirled this way and that, desperate to find some rational cause, but there simply was none; his new home had been invaded, and by a person or persons invisible. He shrank from the noise, making a rather perfunctory effort to hide behind his tatty old armchair but this seemed a futile enterprise. He thought about running for the door but dismissed the thought at once. Whatever sprite or goblin had invaded his new home, he was sure it would catch him before he could make it to safety; he was, after all, hardly the most athletic of men. And so, with mounting horror, he remained where he was - on his hands and knees, half-obscured behind some very second-hand furniture - while his supernatural tormentor rustled its skirts, laughed its laughs, and said nothing.

Then, all upon a sudden, this sound too ceased without warning and Mr. Preston was once more left alone. Yet our hero, as thankful as he was that this nocturnal visitor seemed to have left, was astute enough to understand that events such as these do not come by twos. The rules of theatre demanded a third act - a climax.

And here it was! As Mr. Preston watched, there appeared before him a ball of light, floating in front of the window and hovering three feet from the floor. It was something akin to a will 'o the wisp except that it seemed to be guided by some controlling intelligence as it moved quickly hither and thither, flitting between the four corners of the room before finally settling back in its place by the window. Despite his mounting terror, Mr. Preston - ever conscious of safety - was becoming concerned about the possibility that the curtains would catch alight, but before he could do anything, the little ball of light expanded, pushing out in all three dimensions until it had assumed - to Mr. Preston's understandable surprise - the shape of a young girl of around eighteen. She was a pretty thing; white porcelain skin and a pleasantly plump face with full lips and a slightly upturned nose. Tight ringlets of hair lightly brushed shoulders left tantalisingly bare by a velvet evening dress in a style fashionable perhaps a decade earlier. There was, however, no doubt that she was not real. This was made most clear by the fact that she was monochrome, her features picked out in sharp sepia tones, but also that she *glowed* as if lit from within by some luminescence and (last but by no means least) the fact that as our hero watched she flickered, her image warping and breaking up at intervals; indeed, had this incident occurred a decade or two later, perhaps, one might have said that Mr. Preston was put in mind of the celluloid delights of the local picture palace.

The girl was laughing, but no sound issued from her mouth. This part of the performance, it seemed, was to be a dumb-show. Still laughing, she began to dance; her animal urges given agency in a simplistic, jerky, but somehow joyous expression of sheer delight. She was, Mr. Preston noted, carrying something in her right hand - a scrap of paper that she clutched to her breast as she whirled. A love-note? It seemed likely given her obvious happiness. Yes, happiness - the air of the room suddenly seemed suffused with it, the atmosphere a heady mix of spices that warmed Mr. Preston and filled his heart with gladness. Suddenly, he realised, he was not scared. He felt a pull - an urge to leap from his hiding place and grasp this delightful girl in his arms and embrace her, to celebrate with her, to make her joy his own. The rational side of his brain remained afraid, uncomprehending, aware that this was a monstrous breach of the laws of nature and God. But what did that matter? Nothing that felt this intoxicating, this beautiful could cause him any harm.

But just as Mr. Preston was about to spring forth and join in the dance, a sensation of a quite different nature descended upon him. It came like an icy finger at the base of his spine, running up his back until it clutched at his throat. Something had intruded upon the happy scene; some sense of intense evil that lurked in the corners of the room like a malign mold growing upon the wooden panels. The girl danced on, seemingly unaware, but the atmosphere of the room had, in a trice, changed utterly. A feeling of dread rising in him like bile, Mr. Preston turned his head and saw some flickering shadow spring from the corner, barely visible in the moonlight from the window. It grew in jerky, mechanical movements like some great raven slowly opening its wings until it had assumed the shape of a man. He was around six feet in height, but appeared shorter as he crept, hunched, around the perimeter of the room. Mr. Preston could not see him clearly, but he formed an impression of glowering, coal-black eyes and a downturned, cruel mouth. His heart thumping, Mr. Preston looked back to the young girl to find her dancing still, unaware of the intruder. He felt an urge to scream, to warn her, to stop the horrible conclusion toward which this situation seemed to be advancing inexorably, but his voice had left him. He was part of the dumb-show now, helpless to intervene even if the girl could have heard him through the years which separated them.

And then the girl too caught sight of the intruder. She screamed a soundless scream as he bounded silently toward her, and...

Oh, dear reader, I shall not tell you what Mr. Preston witnessed that night. It was a horrible thing to be sure, and that pretty young girl with her dancing and her love-notes suffered horribly before the end which came, in the end, swiftly and mercilessly. And then that horrible raven stood over his kill, breathing heavily and still in a state of some considerable excitement as the luminescence from his quarry faltered and dimmed, before finally going out altogether and plunging Mr. Preston, the room and the world into a blackness all the darker for what it had just witnessed.

* * * * *

The next morning, Mr. Preston awoke - still lying behind the armchair where he had swooned after his experiences. He stood up, stretched stiffly, and then made his way to the tiny kitchen where he (with some considerable effort and not a few broken eggshells) made himself breakfast and a cup of tea. Having finished that, he went out and bought himself a copy of the Times, which he took back to his rooms to read. And finally, having exhausted all avenues in terms of distracting himself from his situation, he sat at the kitchen table and cried for around an hour. Once he had done that, he pulled on his biggest coat, packed a few things into an overnight bag, took a cab to the station (by way of the telegraph office) and boarded the second-class compartment of a train heading in the direction of the Yorkshire coast.

A few hours later, he was sitting in a small cafe overlooking the sea in the town of Scarborough. The town, quite out of season of course, was quiet and imparted a feeling of splendid isolation; of being a place that had lost its purpose and was having to make some considerable effort not to succumb to the effects of entropy and simply crumble and fall into the sea. Overhead skies full of dark clouds roiled in the way such clouds are wont, and through the window of the little cafe Mr. Preston could see the sea lapping hungrily against the shore in great waves, while around the curve of the bay and upon the high cliff top the ruins of a great castle sat like a silent watchman. With the Punch and Judy men gone and the pleasure palaces closed for the winter, this was not a place in any danger of offering succor to the kind of man who might be recovering from a traumatic experience of the luridly gothic sort.

But the cafe was warm and cosy and the tea and scones were sweet, so Mr. Preston stayed and by-and-by was joined by another. This was his great friend Dodds - the pair had been undergraduates together at Oxford and had become firm friends based on little more than the fact that Preston was intelligent and Dodds was attractive to women. And so, like some lumbering gestalt, they had progressed together through college life, passing their exams (thanks to Preston) and enjoying a full and rewarding social life (thanks to Dodds). Their studies concluded, there had been talk that they would move to the capital together, try to find work with the same firm and engage in the giddy social whirl of London life. These plans, as plans so often do, fell apart when Dodds' father was carried off by a bout of the flu, leaving his only son and heir with a substantial property on the North Yorkshire coast and a considerably less substantial income. Maintaining the former in the face of the latter was no small task, and the pair had somewhat drifted apart in recent years as Preston had built a career, married and had children and Dodds had done whatever it is that a man in his position does. Nevertheless, Mr. Preston still considered this man his one true friend and indeed, he was the only person who had not deserted him when the scandal of his gambling debts had become public knowledge.

"Well?" said Dodds after a considerable pause. "What is the meaning of waking me at such an ungodly hour? I had been out making merry last night, and an urgent telegram is - as I am sure you well know - not what one needs the morning after one has been out making merry!"

With that, he sat down and helped himself to a piece of scone from the little plate in front of his friend, raising an eyebrow appreciatively as he bit into it. Dodds was a year older than his friend but could have quite easily passed for a decade younger; long, sandy-blonde hair fell across his grey eyes and his brow, which sat atop a sharp, hawk-like nose and a mouth just the right size and shape for smiling at girls, was unlined by the years.

So Mr. Preston poured out his tale, beginning with his meeting with Mr. Moorcock and ending with his journey to Scarborough. Through it all Dodds ate his friend's scones, drank his friend's tea and nodded at the appropriate moments. Then, the story finished, he laughed uproariously. "Well, my old friend," he said when his merriment subsided, "I must admit, when I got your telegram this was not what I was expecting. I thought you were going to tell me that dreary bloody marriage of yours was finally over!"

Mr. Preston did not rise to this, because he had expected no less. Dodds bore little respect for the great and noble institution of marriage and had always barely tolerated Preston's wife. Still, it hurt to hear his own union subjected to such a withering assessment. He shrugged. "I have come to you because you are my only friend. I am totally ruined, and it was a severe enough shock to find myself living in such circumstances at all but this... this is quite beyond, Dodds. I cannot go back to that house ever again, yet I have signed a contract. Where else am I to go? I hate to impose on so good and old a friend as you but you can see I really have no choice."

Dodds poured the last cup of tea in the pot, took it for himself and swirled it contemplatively. "So you want to stay with me? It's a dull old life here, Preston, make no mistake. Are you really to be forced out of London by some spook?" He sipped his tea and thought for a moment. "I want to see it myself," he said eventually.

Mr. Preston gasped. "See it? But Dodds, it's horrible! I could not imagine for a moment why anyone should wish to see such an ugly spectacle as I have described."

Dodds shrugged. "Call it a morbid curiosity. I've always been fascinated by these things, this seems like an excellent opportunity doesn't it?"

Preston leaned forward and whispered. "But this isn't just rattling chains and rapping on tables, Dodds. I don't think I could stand it even if it was just that but this is so much worse..."

"Nevertheless, I want to see. I'm quite firm, Preston. Or perhaps you don't want me to see because there's nothing to see - perhaps you've made the whole thing up, or you've turned to drink."

Mr. Preston appeared scandalised. "I tell you no! Can you really think such a thing, Dodds, and us being such old friends?"

"Well," said Dodds, smiling reassuringly, "Here's what we're going to do. We are going to go back to London - both of us - immediately. I'm going to see your ghost. Then, I will help you decide what to do. And don't worry so - you're welcome to barricade yourself in the bedroom if you wish. I have no interest in forcing you to sit through the wretched thing again if you don't want to. We've been friends a long time, Sam. I wouldn't do that to you. But if, once I've seen what's what, we both decide that the best course is for you to come and live here for a while, then that can easily be arranged. One night, Preston. Give me one night."

So, though he knew in his heart he ought not, Mr. Preston dejectedly agreed. And once again, reader, I am minded to add the words "would that he had not".

* * * * *

Dodds was too excited to return home and pack, and so after taking the little tramway up the hill into the town the pair was soon puffing their way back southwards. On the train, Dodds made repeated attempts at jovial conversation but his companion remained taciturn and uncommunicative. Mr. Preston was finding it hard to concentrate; he was far too concerned with the idea of going back to those rooms. His stomach churned, and his mind fixated on some unseen threat; some promise of disaster if he followed this course. Why had he done it? He wasn't certain, even now. Perhaps he had agreed to Dodds' suggestion because, deep down in his heart, he wanted some confirmation that he wasn't imagining it. That he was not losing his mind as a result of his self-created misfortunes of late. And yet there was something, some corner of his mind that would not stop picking at his consciousness. It was like a dark bird had lodged within him, cawing out its ill-starred words to him and him only, pecking away bit-by-bit at his sanity. At himself.

At that moment, Dodds made some facile remark and Preston looked up, meaning only to nod or otherwise signal that he was still listening to his friend (though of course he was not) when he saw, out in the corridor beyond their compartment, a dark shadow pass. It was only there for the most fleeting of moments - yet he felt somehow, in some way he could not readily articulate, that he knew what it was. He staggered to his feet and, to the evident surprise of Dodds, he threw open the compartment door. The corridor outside was empty. But Mr. Preston was not to be put off - he peered into the next compartment, causing the elderly spinster occupying it to glare at him in a particularly affronted manner. He moved on to the next one. No, nothing to be seen there either. He was about to move through the door into the next carriage and continue his search when he felt a hand upon his shoulder and whirled around to see Dodds smiling at him.

"What is it, old chap?" smiled his friend. And what could Mr. Preston say? That he feared for his sanity? That he had been chasing a shadow? A ghost? He shook his head and replied that he thought he needed a lie down. Dodds escorted him back to their compartment and nothing further passed between the pair until the lumbering iron giant bearing them hissed into their station.

* * * * *

Dodds paid for the cab back to Preston's rooms, reasoning (correctly) that his jaunt to the coast had severely depleted his friends few remaining funds. Once there, Preston insisted on preparing a light supper for the pair (which Dodds ate with good humour despite his friend's culinary skills being of the standard one would expect from a man who had until recently had the wherewithal to employ a cook). Then Mr. Preston announced that he was off to bed, that he would be locking the door and that if Dodds decided he wanted to call off this insanity then he should knock on the bedroom door and the pair would flee the house and wander the streets until morning. Dodds, laughing, said that there was no need for Mr. Preston to worry and that he would be fine in the armchair by the fire. The matter settled, Dodds pulled a slim volume from the bookshelf and settled in for the night.

* * * * *

Tucked up tightly beneath the covers and with the door securely locked (and wedged shut with a chair for good measure) Mr Preston spent the night sleeping fitfully, but without any great disturbance. As to what was happening to Dodds he did not know but though he woke at regular intervals he neither saw nor heard anything amiss, and at length he began to worry that perhaps the dumb-show had not played tonight. Of course, who was to say when or how regularly the haunting manifested? Nobody, least of all Mr. Preston, truly understood such matters, did they? Did the supernatural keep to a schedule? If not, what would Dodds think? Mr. Preston was already acutely aware of the possibility that his friend would think he had simply imagined the whole thing.

    Then another thought came unbidden into his mind - what if the haunting had come at the appointed hour only to scare Dodds so out of his wits that he had left, and that now Mr. Preston was here all alone? Now that was a terrible thought to be sure, but to go out of the room to check. That would have been worse. So Mr. Preston stayed precisely where he was, keeping the covers over his head like a child warding off the monster in the wardrobe, and waited until morning.

* * * * *

It was late enough by the time that Mr. Preston awoke that the cold winter sun was cresting the tops of the houses in the district. He prised open a gluey eye and looked around to ensure everything was as he expected it to be before he climbed tentatively from his bed, threw on a shirt and a pair of trousers and removed the chair he had been using to secure the door. He padded slowly into the living room where he found Dodds - already wide awake and pacing the room in a state of high excitement.

"Sam!" called out Dodds. "You wouldn't believe it! Well, you probably would. It happened again! Right on the stroke of three, exactly as you said! It was horrible!"

Mr. Preston nodded dumbly. "Yes, it is, isn't it? So now can we go? You've seen what you wanted, after all."

But Dodds shook his head. "Not yet, old friend. First, I need to make a little proposal. Get yourself washed and dressed, and give me a lend of some clothes. Then we'll go out for breakfast. My treat."

* * * * *

So go out for breakfast they did. Dodds ate fast and talked faster - both men had clearly been affected by the events afoot in the wee hours but where Mr. Preston had become sullen, introverted and anxious his friend was manic, excitable. He ran through the details of what he had seen again and again, in more and more lurid detail. Mr. Preston, who had already lived through this once and was not in the mood for any more repeat performances, put up a hand to stop the unstoppable verbal flow. "Well?" he said. "We're here because you said you had a proposal. What is it?"

Dodds smiled broadly and bit the end from the sausage he was brandishing on the end of his fork. Then he took a large gulp of coffee and threw his arms wide. "There's an opportunity here, Sam!" he laughed. "An unbelievable opportunity and you nearly missed it." He sat back and composed himself, pushing the hair from his eyes and rubbing the bridge of his nose thoughtfully. "Okay, think back a few years. You remember those American girls, the... Fox sisters, I think it was. Then there was that Hayden woman, the table-rapper. You remember? She made a fortune, Sam! London is awash with phoney mediums pulling a sheet of muslin out of their bloody mouths and telling a load of credulous idiots that it's ectoplasm. And they're all rich! The people in this city are gripped by a mania for the afterlife, for ghosts and goblins, for communion with the dead. But everywhere they look all they see is fakery and chicanery. And then there's us. You, I mean. You have the real thing, in your living room, every night, running to a strict schedule. You, Preston, are living in a bloody goldmine."

Now Mr. Preston was not a slow man. He was sharp, intelligent and studious. So that he did not immediately realise what his friend was driving at was not a result of stupidity but rather because what was being suggested was so horrible - so monstrous - that he simply couldn't believe it was being given voice. "So," he began falteringly, "What exactly are you suggesting?"

Dodds breathed in sharply. "I'm saying, if people will pay through the nose for some woman banging on the underside of a table with her knee, what will they pay to see this? A bona-fide haunting? No tricks, not nonsense. Absolutely genuine. It could be the sensation of London."

Appalled, Mr. Preston shook his head vigorously. "But you can't be serious! To charge people to see such horrors is immoral beyond belief. I won't do it!"

Dodds sat back and sighed. "Immoral? How many people in this city make their money immorally? The slum landlords? The moneylenders? The men who sell women's virtue, or opium, or who cut purses and pick pockets? The bankers, the politicians, the warmongers and - lest we forget - the bookmakers? They revel in human misery and profit by it. Now you can swim against the tide until you are carried off and drowned, or you can join in and make some money. Real money. The kind of money that can rebuild your reputation, get your career back on track and - who knows? - maybe fix things between you and that wife you seem so attached to."

And that, reader, was that. For a few moments more Mr. Preston, scandalised and horrified, blustered and railed against the idea but the seed was planted. The idea that these terrible events could somehow be turned to his advantage, that he could put his life back together... well that created a pull, an urge in Mr. Preston which Dodds knew full well would overcome any objection. And so it proved, as a visibly worn-down and weary Preston finally gave in.

And so the plot was hatched - Dodds would make all the arrangements; he had previously been a member of a good London club and still kept in touch with some of the other members among whom he believed there were a number with plenty of money, less sense and a modish interest in all things supernatural. He would put the word about among them and encourage them to spread it among like-minded friends. Mr. Preston's role would be simpler - to keep the house presentable, welcome the guests, serve a few drinks and - most important of all - ensure that the landlord, Mr. Moorcock, did not get wind of what they were doing. If he did, said Dodds, there was a risk that he may (as the owner of the property) insist on a cut of the profits. That aside, Preston was welcome to stay out of the way during the 'performances'.

And so, Dodds and a rather conflicted Preston walked back through the snow, now melting in the midday sun, back toward the premises of their new venture. Preston smiled and nodded as his friend gabbled excitedly about the scale of the opportunity they had been presented with and how rich Mr. Preston could become. But what occupied Mr. Preston was not his imminent wealth but the inescapable sensation that he was being watched. The tangible feeling of two dark eyes boring into the back of his skull was tangible, yet when he turned, it was to the view of a rather pathetic looking and elderly dachshund staring forlornly at him through rheumy eyes. That aside, the street was quite empty.

* * * * *

At Mr. Preston's insistence it was decided that the pair would not stay overnight in the haunted rooms, though Dodds was plain that for the sake of appearances it would be necessary for Preston to spend at least some time there lest the other tenants or Mr. Moorcock had their suspicions aroused. Instead, at the expense of Dodds, they booked into a local hotel, the best one in the district though the rooms were neither particularly large nor particularly clean. They passed a comfortable and refreshing night and the next morning enjoyed a well-cooked breakfast, before Dodds announced that he had to go into the city to meet with some people. Dutifully Mr. Preston returned home, with some trepidation for this was his first time spent there alone since he had left for Scarborough, but on returning he found the atmosphere quite pleasant just as it had been on his fateful first visit with Mr. Moorcock. He rearranged the furniture a little, left a few things out on the breakfast table to make the place appear lived-in and on having completed his work to a satisfactory degree he left, making sure that he was seen by his neighbour, an ancient crone by the name of Mrs. Prendergast. Then he made his way to one of the larger London parks where he spent a thoroughly pleasant afternoon watching the children play and the young lovers walk arm-in-arm. To be those people! To be the person he himself had been not so very long ago; young and in love, with no debtors chasing him and no supernatural horrors lurking around every corner. He realised how much he had loved his simple life, and how much he longed to have it back. That was why he was going along with this lunatic scheme of Dodds - the merest hint that all was not lost, that things could again be the way they were, that the things he had experienced could have a happy outcome... it was more than he could ever have hoped. Perhaps Dodds was right, perhaps the whole thing would go swimmingly and he could pay off his debts and buy a new house in a good part of town and get back his position in the firm and, that done, that he could reconcile with his wife, the only woman he had ever loved. This was all he could think of, all that kept the threads of his sanity bound. For the first time in a long time, he began to feel a genuine optimism about the future. Even the strange sensation of being watched that had dogged him for the last few days had gone. He was as at peace with the world as he could have been given his situation.

So it was not an at all unhappy Mr. Preston who strolled into his hotel in the late afternoon as the darkness was beginning to descend on the city. He pulled off his gloves and approached the desk to ask if Mr. Dodds had yet returned but the elderly clerk shook his head. "He did come back, sir, but only to settle the bill and to say that he and you would not be needing the room again tonight. He left a note for you, sir."

Anxiously, Preston took the folded scrap of paper and flipped it open. In Dodds' spidery hand was written a greeting and an explanation that things had moved faster than he had expected.

The show would go on - that very night - and the pair was to rendezvous at midnight in order to prepare for their guests.

* * * * *

Dodds was waiting by the front door smoking when Preston rounded the corner a few minutes before midnight. Wordlessly the pair entered the building and went up to Preston's rooms. Dodds had brought with him a few bottles - brandy and port chiefly - with which to serve the guests. "You wouldn't have believed it," he laughed as he and Preston tidied the living room and built a good-sized fire. "The words were hardly out of my mouth before I had half a dozen people wanting to come this very night. Absolutely desperate, they were, willing to pay any price. We settled on twenty guineas apiece, is that all right? Oh, one or two wanted to bring their lady friends along for a bit of a thrill so they're paying double."

Mr. Preston was quite taken aback. Twenty guineas was an extraordinary sum for someone to pay for such a gaudy entertainment - there were a good number of people in London for whom that was an entire year's wage. That was when the thought struck him; he was going to be rich! Not merely 'comfortably off' as he had been for most of his life, he could become extremely wealthy out of this opportunity which had so unexpectedly been thrown his way. Why, if what Dodds had told him were at all accurate then this one night alone would clear his outstanding debts a dozen times over! There would be no need to return to his job, no need to work at all. It was a strange realisation, that the means of his salvation should come from so horrid a source, but had his wife not always said 'The good Lord shall provide'?

And then, suddenly, Mr. Preston had a horrible thought. "I say, Dodds," he stammered. "How much of a cut do you want from this?"

Dodds looked affronted. He stopped what he was doing and turned to his friend. "Why, whatever makes you ask such a thing? Look, we're friends aren't we? All I want is to feel that I've been able to do you a good turn. I'll take a few pounds to cover the cost of the hotel and the train journeys but otherwise the money is all yours. I couldn't take a penny from you, not with you being in the situation you are."

Mr Preston smiled and put a hand on his friend's shoulder. "Thank you," he smiled. "You really are a true and constant friend."

Dodds merely shrugged. "Why, it is - I would imagine - no more than you would do for me. But listen, can I offer you one bit of advice? Don't put your money from this little venture into the bank - not to begin with at any rate. Might raise some questions, a man in your position suddenly making such large deposits. No, what you should do is get yourself a nice solid strongbox or something of the kind, and leave it right here. Where we can both keep an eye on it."

Mr. Preston nodded and went back to his work. Within half an hour the place looked about as good as it was ever going to and the pair sat down to await their visitors.

* * * * *

At two, the visitors began to arrive. Each slipped in with a smile and a wave to Dodds, and Preston took their hats and coats and directed them through to the living room where they were offered drinks. As Dodds had said, several of the men brought their lady friends, and the females of the company appeared agitated and on edge but - as the spirits flowed - the men folk became more relaxed and jovial. This was partly the work of Dodds who was circulating the room keeping the conversation flowing. Nobody spoke to Mr. Preston, who hung in the background as though he himself were a ghost, springing into action only when a glass needed refilling.

When the third hour of the morning was almost at hand, Mr. Preston took Dodds aside and whispered quietly that he would rather not be present for what was about to happen. Dodds shrugged and turned back to his conversation so Mr. Preston took himself off to his bedroom and - as he had before - he locked the door, wedged it shut and sat on the edge of the bed. He sat for a little while until he heard the distant church clock softly strike the third hour. And then Mr. Preston pulled his knees into his chest, rocked himself gently back and forth, and waited to see what would happen.

For a while, there was nothing. Now at first Mr. Preston felt comforted by this, but it soon occurred to him that if the haunting did not play at its appointed hour then the customers would undoubtedly refuse to pay their twenty guineas and the whole thing would be for naught. But just as the spectre of further reputational and fiscal damage raised its ghastly head he heard a scream - loud and piercing - from outside his door. He checked his watch - it was now a quarter past the hour, just the time that the grisly spectacle should be ending. He threw open his door and marched into the living room to a scene so appalling he could scarcely bring himself to think of it afterwards.

One of the women was hysterical - lying on the floor and refusing to move or to do anything but issue a series of long, loud moans. She was being comforted by the two other women present who each looked up at him as he entered, their faces chalk-white and their eyes wide with shock. This was no more than Mr. Preston expected. What was truly horrible was the sight of Dodds with the other men of the company, each of whom held a glass of brandy in one hand, a cigar in the other and each of whom, furthermore, was laughing uproariously as if they had recently seen the funniest thing of their entire lives. Mr. Preston ignored them and went instead to the aid of the prone woman, taking her hand gently and stroking it. He looked into the eyes of the other women and saw nothing but contempt and naked hatred there, and he knew at once what had provoked it. He had made an entertainment, a sideshow, of the thing they feared the most. Something so fearful to them as to be spoken of only in hushed whispers, and he and Dodds had turned it into a cheap thrill for their boorish men folk who, as the final insult, had made them come along to watch, to make themselves party to this depravity.

"I say, old man," snorted Dodds from his place by the fire. "Couldn't you quieten her down a bit? We don't want the whole neighbourhood being woken."

* * * * *

A half an hour later, the party - men, women and all - had climbed into their carriages and vanished into the night. Preston was left alone with Dodds. He shook his head sadly. "I don't think I can do it anymore," he said. "Those women... I think the look on their faces will haunt me to the grave."

Dodds chuckled. "Don't let it bother you so. We're pushing back the boundaries of human experience here, you have to expect some people not to cope. Besides, you're going to be rich. We've come this far. It would be madness to change our course now. Some of the chaps tonight want to come back again. They're going to tell all their friends. This is going to be a success, Preston, make no mistake."

Mr. Preston shook his head. "But promise me, Dodds. No more women. The sight of that fellow dragging his poor girl away like a sack of spuds tonight was more than I could bear to see again. We will go on, but not women. Not again. They shouldn't have to see this."

Dodds shrugged. "Well it'll impact on the profits, but I suppose it's your money. Fine, Sam. No more women. They're more bloody trouble than they're worth anyway."

* * * * *

So on it went for two weeks. Each night the parade of young men with their well-tailored suits and Oxbridge affectations, each night the crowd being a little larger than the last. Each night Mr. Preston locked himself in his room at the appointed hour and each night he emerged to the same scene, Dodds and his friends drinking and laughing as if this were all some great joke.

However the money poured in, and that was no lie. Piles and piles of the stuff, so that after the fortnight had passed Mr. Preston had a King's ransom locked away in his strongbox. He had never seen so much money - why, he could walk into any district in London and buy a house outright, for cash. He could fill it with furniture and take on a few servants and all with enough left by to live on comfortably for a good many years. For the first few days, Dodds had been out around the town spreading the word but now it was entirely unnecessary, the thing had quite taken on a life of its own and word had spread like a virus among the city's richest folk. Indeed Mr. Preston felt sure he had seen some members of the gentry and even an MP or two, though he never asked for names nor were they proffered. Yet Mr. Preston felt a nagging sensation in his heart. He had done this for one reason and one reason only, and now it was time, he felt, to face that reason head-on.

So it was that he found himself, early one morning after he had had not more than a few hours of broken sleep, pounding the streets of one of the more well-to-do areas of the city looking among the tall, stern-looking townhouses for the home of his sister-in-law. Finally, he located it, and tentatively he climbed the steps and rapped on the black-painted door with his cane.

A moment later the door was prised open a fraction and inside he saw a young girl of no more than eighteen, her hair forced into a tight bun and her rigid posture speaking of a life in service. Taking off his hat, he introduced himself and handed over his card, and the young girl ushered him inside and closed the door. Mr. Preston found himself in a hallway not unlike the one in his own house - his former house that is - with neat black and white tiles forming a chessboard on the floor and a tall plant standing to attention by a hat stand. At the other side of the hallway was a wide flight of richly carpeted stairs and after not so many moments it was from these stairs that a woman in early middle age emerged, her face pinched and her long blonde hair hanging loose around her shoulders.

"She has no interest in seeing you, Samuel," the woman said haughtily. "I am rather afraid you have had a wasted trip, so kindly leave before we have any unfortunate scenes."

But Mr. Preston was not to be put off so easily. "If she would have a divorce, Judith, then that is her choice. But then the matter must be discussed, and it would harm the reputation of your family a good deal less if we could speak between ourselves and behind closed doors rather than air our dirty linen in court. Do you not think?"

Judith glared witheringly at her brother-in-law but eventually stood aside and let him up the steps, though out of spite she did not take his hat and coat or offer him a cup of tea. "The first room on the left," she hissed venomously though gritted teeth.

At the top of the stairs, Mr. Preston found the room and knocked softly. After a few moments it was opened by a woman in her early thirties with mousey brown hair tucked messily into a pony-tail. Her face was lined with worry and an air of defeat seemed settled on her shoulders. She turned away from Mr.

Preston when she saw that it was he, but she did not close the door so Mr. Preston stepped into the room behind her and put a hand on her shoulder. She shrugged it away coldly. "I told Judith I did not wish to see you," she sighed.

Mr. Preston smiled. "You will remember that I was always persistent. Do you remember how I courted you, Lucy? All those years ago. You always said I ground you down with my persistence."

Lucy Preston laughed, sadly. "You ground me down, Samuel, but not in the way you mean. When I think now about the thing I put up with. The things you made me put up with, because I did love you. The times I had to swallow my pride, to borrow money from my family to make ends meet. The times I had to wait in that bank while you begged them not to take our home. And worst of all, the times I had to sit in that house, alone, knowing you were at that racetrack throwing away everything we'd saved for. Everything we'd worked for. And when it all fell down around your ears you ran away and you hid. You're not a man, Samuel. You're a beast. A wicked beast!"

She was shaking now, the adrenaline flowing around her bloodstream as she fought to overcome her naturally quiet nature and get out all the things she had been desperate to say for so long.

Mr. Preston sighed sadly and sat on the edge of the bed, staring at the floor contritely and shuffling his feet. "I know," he said eventually. "I know that what I did was terrible. But I have changed, Lucy. I have."

Lucy laughed. "Oh, you have, have you? Do you have any idea, Samuel, how long ago that stopped working on me?"

"But it's true," whined Mr. Preston. "Dodds and I have gone into business, legitimate business. I haven't been near a bookmaker in weeks. Dodds and I have been making good money, very good. Enough for you and I to try again, to set up in a new home, somewhere we've never lived before where nobody knows us, and just live. Just live, just the two of us in complete solitude until everything is resolved. And then, perhaps, we can try again. You know, for children? It's what you always wanted, Lucy, and now we can finally be stable enough to do it."

But Lucy shivered. "How can I believe a word you say, Samuel? Why would I? After everything you've said, everything you've done. You disgust me, Samuel. And as for your business, with Dodds, don't take me for a fool. The man is a scoundrel, a wastrel and so are you, I don't believe that the two of you could run any kind of business. And even if you could, I'd expect the profits to end up in the gin palaces and the bookmakers before I ever saw a penny."

"But it's true! I would not lie to you, not again. We are running a business, we are making more money than I can spend by myself. So I would have you by my side, to enjoy it with. I want us to put things right."

Lucy sat down and folded her arms. "So just what is this business of yours?"

At this, Mr. Preston looked down at the floor and closed his eyes. "I... I cannot tell you. Not yet."

"And this is it, is it? Your new start? Lies upon lies, as ever Samuel. You've started some mysterious business, in the last two weeks, with Dodds. Neither of you have any capital to speak of yet you have already made more money than you can spend. It's painfully obvious what has happened, Samuel, so please don't insult my intelligence further. You have been gambling again, you have had a substantial win, and now you are here trying to use this money to convince me to come back to you. It is pathetic. YOU are pathetic. The only thing I want from you is a divorce, Samuel, and unless you have come here to discuss it then there is nothing more to be said."

Now if there is anything to be said for Mr. Preston, he was always a man who knew when he was beaten. Without another word, he stood and left. He trudged down the stairs and out of the big black front door, down the steps and out into the road. He thought about hailing a cab, for the day was growing cold, but he realised he had not brought any money out with him. He set off glumly and within half an hour, he was almost back to his rooms. He was passing through a particularly repellant side street, the odour of fresh urine thick in his nostrils, when he was once again gripped by the sensation that he was being watched. He stopped and turned around but just as last time, there was nothing to see; a derelict clutching an empty bottle of gin lay against one wall, insensible, but otherwise nothing stirred under the midday sun.

As he turned to walk on, he felt the sensation again; more strongly this time. He was opposite a narrow alleyway, the shadows falling across the entrance and obscuring all within from view. And yet, Mr. Preston was somehow aware of a shape within the alleyway - a darkness within darkness, picked out in a darker shade against the whirling lagoon of blackness. He had a sense of the shape of a man, crouching furtively. As Mr. Preston watched, transfixed, the shape stood up, flexing its limbs as if waking from a deep sleep, but then the arms began to grow - expanding out until they had assumed the shape of a pair of great black wings like those of a huge raven, brushing the walls of the alley as they flexed outward. From within the face burned two eyes, staring out with a jet-black intensity and a level of hatred Mr. Preston had never before felt. It was hate manifested as a physical force - he felt it like a hand on his chest pushing him away, punching him, choking him. And then all of it - eyes, wings and man - were gone in a trice, and Mr. Preston realised he had not taken a breath since the apparition had appeared. He quickly took a few lungfuls before taking to his heels and running as quickly as he could back to his rooms.

* * * * *

When he arrived, Mr. Preston threw the door shut and turned the key in the lock. He realised he was out of breath and stood for a few moments gathering himself before going through into the living room, where Dodds was sitting with his feet up on the table reading a newspaper.

"Ah," smiled Dodds as he saw his friend enter. "How did your little visit go? No, don't tell me - I can see by your face that it was not a happy encounter. Well I have to tell you, Sam, I too have been out and about this morning. I have met with someone of great interest, someone I have been waiting to meet for some time. I shan't go into detail about who that is, because it isn't anyone you know. But listen, he can possibly put me in touch with some people who might be interested in the service we offer and who might be in a position to put a lot of money our way. But the thing is, old man, it means me being out of town tonight, so you're going to have to take care of our guests. Is that okay?"

Mr. Preston shook his head. "No, I can't. I won't. The whole thing is off, Dodds. I'm sorry. I've made all the money I need and my marriage is over. I am going to take what I have and go; get out of London and far away from this house and its horrors."

With that, Preston sat down with his head in his hands and began to weep. Dodds stirred himself from his seat by the fire and put a consoling hand on his friend's shoulder. "Listen, old man," he said unsteadily. "The thing is... I need to ask you something. The estate's in trouble, you know? I didn't want to say but I need money rather badly and I thought, perhaps, if I could arrange this one last big night, then you might allow me to keep what we make. After all, Sam, I have been good to you. Haven't I? I have been a good friend and helped you when I could. Now I am only asking for the same in return."

Mr. Preston looked up, his eyes red and blotchy. "Why did you not tell me this before? If you need money, I will gladly offer it to you. You can take some of what is in the strongbox. Would twenty pounds be enough? Fifty?"

But Dodds shook his head. "No, Sam, you need that. You have a wonderful new life to plan and to build and you may need every penny of that money. No, please let me do this my way."

"But you are asking me to be here, tonight, and to be present for the whole thing. I can't do it!"

Dodds shrugged. "I do understand that, Sam. I do. But let us not forget that I have been doing just that for the last two weeks. I have been running the show while you have been hiding in the bedroom, and I have never complained or asked for anything from you. Well now, I am asking you this. Please would you help me as I have helped you?"

And what could Mr. Preston say to that? Despite his terror at what was being asked of him, he had only one true friend in all the world and the notion of letting him down or disappointing him was one he simply could not countenance. Against his better judgment, he found himself agreeing.

* * * * *

So there sat Mr. Preston, alone, as the clock struck two. He had prepared the place as best he could - building a decent fire to keep out the cold and ensuring that the supply of spirits was well stocked. Now he simply sat, deathly afraid lest the show should begin early or no guests should arrive, leaving him here, alone, at the third hour of the morning.

But Mr. Preston had not slept well the night before, out of nervousness at the prospect of meeting his wife, and so he slipped gently into a light sleep, until he heard upon the door a sharp rap. He opened an eye and his gaze fell upon the clock on the mantel - and was gripped with panic to realise that it was just five minutes shy of three o' clock. Staggering to his feet, Mr. Preston made his way quickly to the door and opened it. Outside, he saw a man dressed in a long black overcoat. A scarf was wound around his mouth to keep out the cold and he wore on his head a wide-brimmed black hat that cast a shadow over his features. Though he could not see the features of the newcomer, Mr. Preston formed an impression of an older man, of a studious and inquisitive nature. Perhaps a scholar or academic wishing to see a new scientific phenomenon? It mattered little who he was or where his interests lay, for his money was as good as any and so Mr. Preston ushered the man in and held out a hand for his coat, but the man shrugged him off without a word.

"Well," said Mr. Preston as cheerfully as he could manage, "I was expecting a few more people than this. We usually have half a dozen at least, but you are most welcome. Will you take a drink?"

But the man simply shook his head and sat down by the fire. He stared at Mr. Preston in what seemed a disconcerting way, but in truth Preston was glad for the company of even this dour individual as the church clock struck the fateful hour and the show began.

Again, there came that mechanical scratching that was a prelude to the horrors to come. Mr. Preston, with an apologetic smile to his guest, swallowed a large shot of whisky to fortify himself against what he knew was to come. He was not sure he could stand to see this again, but he had promised Dodds and a promise, of course, is a promise. And so the phenomenon went on more-or-less as it had before. The rattling ceased and was followed by the rustle of spectral skirts and the sound of ghostly laughter which gave way, finally, to the horrible dumbshow which Mr.

Preston so feared. He felt the same intoxicating joy fill his heart, but this time it weighed all the more heavily for the foreknowledge of what was to follow. And finally, Mr. Preston screwed his eyes closed, unwilling to witness again the final flickering frames of this drama played out by the horrible carrion bird that had so haunted his waking life and his dreams. And as the final image flickered and faded into nothing, and the atmosphere in the room returned to normal, Mr. Preston realised he was weeping, weeping for a life unfulfilled and a spark of happiness, so precious and rare in this world, that had withered and died at the stroke of a knife.

So when Mr. Preston turned to his companion it was not to offer him a drink or a cigar, or to laugh at the expense of that poor girl and the crude brutality of her end, as Dodds so often had. It was because he wished, just for a moment, to feel a sense of kinship, of comradeship, of something out there, beyond the darkness - a sense of a world which was not a cold place filled with horrors and ghosts and the vengeful men who would break another man's body over a debt unfulfilled. It was because, just for that one fleeting moment, he wanted a feeling of the universe as an interconnected web of spirits, each a bright point filled with compassion and love and a bright, unending light that did not go out but endured and illuminated the world. He wanted to look into that man's eyes and see a flash of something there, something that said, "We shared this, and it was terrible, but things can be better, and they will."

But he didn't see any of that. Instead, he saw that his companion had drawn himself up to is full height, and he had cast off the scarf and the hat. Now Mr. Preston could see that the man was old - perhaps sixty - but that his eyes were alive with coal-black hatred. The man in black began to advance as Mr. Preston realised where he had seen those eyes before. This man was older, of course, but he was undoubtedly the same. "Oh," was all that Mr. Preston could think to say as a sense of horrible finality consumed him. "Oh dear..."

On, inexorably, the man in black came, his back hunched and his arms outstretched, the blade of the knife clasped in his hand appearing red in the light of the dying embers of the fire. He walked with a shuffling, shambling quality that spoke of his advanced years but there was determination there, too. A sense of inevitability, of a long-untold story which was about to gain an unexpected post-script.

And as he felt his back bump against the wall, and realised there was nowhere else to go, Mr. Preston uttered in his mind a silent prayer and thought, one last time, of Lucy.

* * * * *

And that, reader, was that. There is, however, a little more that I should perhaps mention. Mr. Preston's funeral was a sparsely attended affair - there was a Mr. Griggs who had been Preston's former employer. Lucy, of course, was there, though she sat at the back. And then there was Dodds and Mr. Moorcock who, at the conclusion of the service, repaired (at Mr. Dodds' insistence) to Mr. Moorcock's office for a final drink and a chat.

"A terrible business, to be sure," said Mr. Moorcock in a voice that suggested he was discussing inclement weather or spoiled milk rather than the brutal murder of a recent acquaintance. "Did the officers speak to you about what happened?"

Dodds shrugged and poured himself a good sized-glass of gin. He took off his gloves and swirled the greasy fluid around the glass before taking a sip. "Not much, only what I assume was a matter of public record anyway. Poor Samuel was stabbed seventeen times, his throat cut so fiercely that his head was almost severed from his body and his corpse hurled from the window so that it was impaled on the railings below. I believe it was the butcher's boy on his morning rounds who found him. He'll be having nightmares for a while, I suppose."

Mr. Moorcock sighed. "What makes a man do it, do you think, sir?"

But Dodds just swirled his drink and looked at the floor; if he had an answer, Mr. Moorcock never heard it. Instead, when he spoke at last, it was on an entirely different subject.

"I don't suppose," he said, "that you have a key to Samuel's apartment? There are some things there, just a few knick-knacks of little financial value, but I would rather like to have them. To remember him by?"

Mr. Moorcock shrugged. "I think the police took a lot of the stuff in there, sir, as evidence. But you're welcome to whatever you find. Anything you take will save me having to remove it before I can find another tenant." With that, he reached into a large pile of keys on his desk and selected the appropriate one, identifying it by the white tag tied to the end. He tossed the key to Dodds. "You do as you please, sir, only let me have the key back when you're finished."

So it was that Mr. Dodds found himself back in those benighted rooms that morning. He headed straight to the bedroom, prised up the appropriate floorboard and smiled to himself when he saw the strongbox of Samuel Preston still in its hiding place, undisturbed by the attentions of the great Metropolitan Police Force. From his pocket he took the extra key which he had had cut without Mr. Preston's knowledge, opened the box, stuffed the banknotes within into the pockets of his jacket and stood up, leaving the box and the loose floorboard lying where they fell. That done he had a last look around the place, shivered, and left - locking the door securely after him. On his way down, because he was a good friend and true, he made sure to tip his hat as he passed the railing on which Mr. Preston had breathed his last, then he passed into the streets of the capital and disappeared, swallowed up amid the great writhing sea of humanity.

The Specimen
Jodie van de Wetering

Months ago in the post grad office, Milparinka sounded remote and romantic: the sort of place a man could go to make his name, or at least pad out his thesis. Now Matt might as well be on one of the lesser-known moons of Jupiter. Through the windscreen, patches of sage-grey saltbush dot the rocky red dirt stretching out from the single lane of bitumen draped dead-straight across the Outback. His borrowed camper trailer snakes like it's trying to catch its own tail if he goes over 70 miles an hour, so he eases back on the throttle and watches the endless scrub roll by.

  A long-abandoned car gives Matt an excuse to stop and stretch his legs. It's just a few feet from the road, as though the owner stopped for a smoke and forgot to come back. Every trace of paint has long since been scoured away by dust and fire, leaving its 50s pin-up curves the same rusty red as the earth slowly claiming it. Matt circles the car, grey-dry grass crunching under his boots. He lightly runs his fingers over one wheel arch. The oxidised metal crumbles at his touch, giving way and showering the dirt below with flakes of rust. Matt snatches his hand away like he's been stung. He brushes the rust off onto his shorts, and climbs back into the Hilux. As he pulls away, he gives the old car one last look in the rear view mirror. One door hangs open in a final indignity.

  The camper trailer folds out like a pop-up book left open under the gum trees. To the east, the vague pink blush deepens orange by the moment. Matt only has a few hours in the early morning before the October heat drives him back to camp until evening. The net swings neatly left right left right brushing through the saltbush, collecting the soon-to-be-catalogued creatures that make their homes there. Already sweat is running down his face, spreading in fractal patterns across his shirt, sticking the fine dust to his legs.

The heat of day forces Matt back under the canvas lean-to of his camp, sorting through his catch. He delicately removes each little brown moth from the net, delivering a stunning squeeze to the thorax with his forceps before dropping them into the killing jar. This is an act of expedience, not clemency: still conscious, they might damage their wing scales as they thrash in their death throes, rendering themselves less than perfect specimens. A couple of mites join the collection, some aphids, a few little black beetles apparently the same but promising dozens of interesting abdominal variations. For the first time since the post grad office, Matt feels the frisson that led him here, the thrill of holding in his sweaty palm a tiny creature utterly unknown to science. Whatever mysteries this patch of scrub holds are his - his to discover, his to describe, his to rescue from chaos and mount gently on the setting board of order.

One last beetle struggles in the deepest recesses of the net. The dark, shiny creature vigorously dodges the forceps, inch-long body burrowing deeper into the loose mesh. Matt finally grabs it and holds it up to the light.

It is beautiful. It is like nothing he's ever seen.

In sunlight iridescent purple dances across the glossy carapace, shot through with a fine red pattern like the daintiest of calligraphy painted with the smallest of weasel-hair paintbrushes. The pattern loops and curls, so intricate and deliberate Matt almost believes that with the right lens, under the right light, he'd be able to make out words and diagrams in its gleaming wing covers.

Matt reaches for a fresh killing jar, but stops. He wants to take this one back alive. He snatches up a specimen jar instead and slips the beetle inside. He crumples a wad of tissue and dampens it from his precious supply of drinking water and drops into the jar to provide the strange beetle moisture and cover. He ducks out into the sun – like walking into an oven, for all that it's not yet ten in the morning – and strips a few handfuls of saltbush and tips them in as well. Something about the formation of the beetle's mouthparts gives it a resigned air, as though it were disappointed in Matt but not surprised. It steps onto a saltbush twig graciously as a debutante descending the ballroom staircase, and rocks back and forth very slowly on long legs.

Evening, and Matt and his net are busy again. He sweeps through the saltbush as the purple twilight deepens to night. Moths swarm around his headlamp. He waves the insects away from his eyes and spits out one that flew into his mouth during a yawn timed badly for both of them. To get a break from the bombardment he snaps off the light and is instantly swallowed by the darkness. Above him, the Milky Way scrolls across the sky in her own good time, the stars brilliantly clear in the thin air. Somewhere in the far distance, an owl screams. The slow, deliberate thud of a passing kangaroo. His own breath, the only human noise, sounds unnaturally loud.

Creeping cold and a full net send him back to camp. Matt tugs down the insect netting around the lean-to to keep out the hordes of extra visitors attracted by his lantern while he sorts and euthanizes his evening collection. While the killing jars do their work he pulls off his boots and sweaty work wear, swapping them for the thick socks and thermals the night demands. One hand on the lantern's kill switch, he takes a last look at the beetle still rocking gently in its jar. He flicks off the lantern and slumps down in his sleeping bag. He seems to see the filigree across the strange insect's wings glow red in the darkness.

The next day, and the beetle still rocks back and forth as it watches its captor fumble out of the sleeping bag and pull on his boots, swapping one set of protective layers for another. Matt adds some fresh water to its tissue and feels strangely sorry for it in its glass prison. Is he imagining it or is it rocking faster than yesterday, as though the tempo of whatever strange music it danced to was increasing?

Ten o'clock. Only ten? Matt shakes his head to clear it. He's behind schedule. Most of the morning's catch is still in the killing jars awaiting examination. A fly lands on his face and he waves it away without thinking. Somehow the wave never makes it from brain to hand, and the fly marches on until it tickles the corner of his mouth and Matt wipes his face against his shoulder in disgust. He looks down. Both his hands are occupied with his net and forceps, yet for a strange moment he'd imagined a second set of arms free to wave off flies and wipe the sweat from his face. The illusion vanishes in an instant, slipping away like wind through gum leaves.

Four o'clock in the afternoon. At last, the morning's catch is nearly done. The final specimen is an unassuming little aphid known to Matt's paperwork as #21293.

No. Wait. There's already a #21293 listed.

Matt blinks in confusion. Numbers dart around the paper like moths bashing themselves against a light. Rivulets of sweat sting his eyes, making it harder to focus as the numbers buzz and bomb around the page. He reaches for the forceps to grab the numbers and squeeze their thoraces to quieten them before he realises what he's doing and stops dead.

He slowly puts the forceps down. He looks around furtively, as though someone might have seen his folly deep in the scrub. Another sharp blink clears his vision.

He skims back through his day's notes, but the logging numbers are jumbled and chaotic. This is hopeless. A sick feeling rises in his stomach. He flicks back through the pages, shocked by the quantity of notes he's taken in just three days.

Three?

The date headers suggested five.

Matt staggers to his feet. He circles round to the cabin of the ute and sticks his head through the open driver's window. The fuel gauge suggests five days' worth of travel. So does his food stash, and the quantity of water missing from the jerrycans. There is no sense of time out here, and without human activity to set a metronome, the days unravel into an unmeasurable infinity. Over the course of a lifetime, time could wash the days smooth and unchanging – but in five days? Surely he couldn't lose it in five days?

He wakes not remembering lying down to sleep. The first hint of morning colour creeps into a dark sky that seems to be a long, long way away. There's something he should be doing. He can't remember what. It doesn't bother him that he can't remember, but it bothers him that it doesn't bother him, like some important part of himself has been mislaid while he was watching pink and orange creep across the sky.

The beetle hasn't moved. It still rocks back and forth, now noticeably faster than the day before. Matt fumbles with his phone, dropping it and staring at it as it falls, wondering why a limb he doesn't have didn't reach out and catch it. He rescues his phone from the fine dust. It is suddenly important, terribly important, that he quantify the speed of the beetle's steady, deliberate motions. He tries to count how many time the insect rocks in a minute, but watching the timer while trying to count makes the number dart away and crash against the inside of his skull. He hurls the phone to the ground in frustration. It bounces and skitters across the stones into the harsh sunlight.

How is the sun so high already?

Matt looks out at his phone smashed on the rocky ground. He sees... things. Things on the horizon. Red patterns dance and curl to a slowly building rhythm, telling him indescribable, beautiful, terrible things.

He sets off towards them.

It's dark when he returns to camp, his wanderings having described a wide, crooked spiral that led eventually back where he began. He vaguely knows he needs water but can't remember where to find it. Bottles? Jerrycans? Or is it stored on crumpled tissue and the underside of leaves? He reels around the camp. The beetle looks at him. Its rocking is laced with something akin to expectation. He opens the lid. The beetle doesn't move.

But it can, if it wants.

He wakes early again, to the scent of gums and dust and purple clouds blossoming across the sky like a bruise. He feels better than he had in days, even if his head is thick and he's still unsure about his inventory of limbs. He clambers to his feet and looks across the camp. He sees himself snoring in the corner, unshaven face and gangly limbs wrapped in sleeping bag and blanket. Somewhere in the back of his mind he knows he should find that strange, but he can't muster any emotion at the sight of his own slumbering husk. He picks his way deftly along the saltbush twig and up to the lip of the jar. He sniffs the air with senses at once intimate and unfamiliar.

People.

He needs people, for a purpose he doesn't yet entirely understand. He picks up the scent of sweat and sausages from a camp in the distance. Maybe 20 kilometres away. Not more than a day's travel.

He spreads his purple wings, and takes flight.

The Citizen
Hannah G. Parry

The guillotine lives just around the corner. It has been living there for over a year now, a year of what they call the Reign of Terror.

My shop is a carpenter's shop. I rent it, and my rooms above, from a middle-aged widow whose husband once used the building for his grocery business. He died five years ago, before the Bastille was stormed and the world changed forever. I think he died peacefully.

They don't die peacefully, around the corner. I never go to see them – if I have to walk past that street, I do it quickly – but I can hear the noises. The crowds roar and jeer, and the blade sings and then thuds as it goes up and down, over and over again. I try not to think about the bodies, mounting up, filling the air with ghosts. Sometimes, when I hurry past that corner, I see the water in the gutters tinged with blood.

My landlady, Citizeness Michelet, comments on it as she stops by my workshop.

"They've killed five this morning, Citizen Coustier," she says. "All Girondists, I think – nobody I knew. One of them was quite an old man; he needed to be helped up the scaffolding. You should go sometime, Citizen. There's no need to work so hard. And it does the spirit good, to see those heads fall, and know that the country's that much safer."

It is not my fault. It is nothing to do with me. I am a carpenter, not a revolutionary.

I go to work. The rasp of my saw and the blows of my hammer drown out the roar of the crowd.

* * * * *

She comes to me at night, or I go to her.

Her name is Sophia, and she lives in a house in what is now the commune of Montmartre. She's slim – skinny, I could call her, if I were being unkind – and young, about twenty-two. Her face is very pointed and delicate, and her eyes are dark: unusual and striking with her light curls, and the thing that elevates her appearance from ordinary to attractive. That, and her extraordinary capacity to light a room with her smile.

"My gentleman caller," she greets me, as I pass through her door. She shuts it behind me, closing us off from the dark streets outside. "I thought you weren't coming."

"Where else would I go?" I answer, and she grins mischievously, wraps her arms around my neck, and draws my head down into her kiss.

I never know how I get to her house. I don't know who she is, or how we met. I know her name because I heard myself calling her by it, as we lay by the fire one night in her upstairs room. I know where she lives, because I can just see the shadowy Place de Tertre from her window. All I know, though, is going to bed at night, closing my eyes in my bed and opening them to find myself at her door. It's always already opening, and I can feel the faint sting on my knuckles and know that I've knocked. When day breaks, I am back in my bed, as if I've never left; only sometimes not quite in the right place, or with my shoes on. I tell myself she is a dream, but I am never quite sure.

I never know what I'm going to do when Sophia's face appears at the door and glows to see me. I move and feel and respond as one indeed does in a dream – without volition or conscious thought. I hear my voice speak, and I don't recognise it. I take her fiercely in my arms, and I wonder at it even as I can't imagine doing anything else. I love her, I think, although I don't know where that love comes from.

Sometimes, though, she comes to me. By day, or in the grey light of early morning when I open my eyes, I feel her. The shadows in my room or the shop shift, move, and resolve themselves into her form. I see the motion out of the corner of my eye, and I freeze where I am. Only for a moment; then I keep moving, eyes resolutely ahead, not looking. I don't want to see her then.

I would rather go to her. When I go to her, I become a ghost to myself. That's less terrifying than being haunted by one.

"There was a boy I knew once, when I was seven," Sophia says dreamily.

We're lying in a tangle of sheets while the breeze teases us through the window; outside, I can see stars about the dark cut-out shadows of the surrounding houses, and that's all I want to see.

"His name was Jean-Paul, I think; maybe it was Jean-Pierre. I can hardly remember. We weren't friends, exactly, but he used to go out at night when everyone else was asleep. To escape, he said. I don't think he ever did anything, and I don't know what he wanted to escape from. But he knew what our street looked like by dark when you were out in the middle of it, not just looking through a window. He'd walked in the moonlight, and felt the wind from the stars in his hair. I've done all that since, of course: it's not so wonderful. It's the same old street, with a risk of breaking your ankle. But I thought it was something special then. I used to sit by him sometimes, and ask him to describe it."

I wait for her to make her point, but Sophia falls silent. I realise eventually that this was all the point she felt compelled to make.

"What happened to him?" I hear myself ask, although I don't really want to know.

She takes a moment to realise she's being spoken to. I hear her shift in the darkness, and when she speaks, she sounds almost as though she's been startled awake.

"Oh... he died," she says. The tone implies that I already knew, or that she is surprised I don't. "When he was ten, I think. I was eleven. I remember my sister telling me. He died of typhoid fever, along with his brother and sister. They lived on nothing in a filthy room, and his father drank."

"I don't want to talk about dead people," I say, irritably.

She laughs. "Why not?" she says. "We live in the company of the dead. All of us, all the time. That's what ghost stories are about. That's what memory is about."

"I don't live in the company of the dead," I say. "I'm alive. You're alive. We're both right here. You and I, alone. Not some dead child from years ago."

"You're so strange sometimes," she says. She kisses me lightly. "Anyone would think you were jealous."

I am, too. Jealous, and possessive. It's strange to me as well. I'm never like that in my waking life.

When I wake, I hear shouts from the streets below. Jeers, and roars. They made those sounds the day they killed the queen. I don't know who they're killing today, and I don't want to.

I sit up in bed, kick off the blankets. I'm exhausted; I always am after I visit Sophia. My heart is a lead weight in my chest, and it pumps lead throughout my body.

"Jacques," a voice says.

I stiffen. Behind me, I feel a rush of cold air: I've left the window open, obviously. I should turn and close it, but I don't move. I can see the shadows moving and flickering out of the corner of my eye.

* * * * *

I look for Sophia's house in the afternoon, as I have been known to do on a fine day when I have little enough work. I know the vague location from what I can see from the window, and so I wander the streets where I can get past the barricades. I don't know why. I'm always relieved not to find it, because it allows me to tell myself that she is a dream only, but I think that I have to look in order to properly not find it. Does that make sense?

It's a nice day for a walk. The sky is clear and the sun glimmers on the rooftops. There's been a sense of fear in the streets for so long that it has become easy to ignore, like a long-accustomed smell in the air. If I don't look at the people who pass me in their red caps, casting furtive, nervous glances my way, I can almost pretend this is the old Paris. I never minded the old Paris, not like some did. I don't ask for much: just for people to leave me alone. The King and Queen certainly did that.

I've almost forgotten what I'm looking for when I turn the corner and, all at once, it's there before me. The house. I've only seen it up close, standing at the door, but I know, without doubt, that it is it. The shade of the walls, the ramshackle way it squeezes between two bigger houses and blossoms into a roof at the top, the tiny second-floor window that I've stood at many times and looked out at – yes, there's the square, and the weather-cock that turns slightly in the breeze.

It's real. It exists in daylight. I feel like a ghost, standing outside it, and like a ghost I do not breathe.

And then, just for second, I see a shape at the window. It is only for a second, and faintly. But my heart jumps, then begins to thunder in my chest. It is a slim figure, with a familiar nose and chin. In that one glance, I see a wisp of curly hair about her face.

I leave, and quickly, not looking up. The guillotine is at work when I walk past the street, and I keep my head determinedly at my feet. Back in my shop, I hammer countless nails into a set of shelves, and let that cover the cheers.

* * * * *

That night, after I close the shop and return upstairs to my room, the shadows follow me up. I know intellectually that they are only shadows, not shapes, but that's no matter. I'm too aware of the potential of each to melt, drip and reform as the figure that haunts me.

What is she? Who?

I close the door behind me, and sit, cradling a candle in my hand. The bed looks so very cold and empty. It is a large bed, meant for two people, and too big for the stunted thing I have become.

Out of the corner of my eye, I see the shadows flicker.

"Jacques," her voice says.

"No," I say, firmly – or would-be firmly. I get to my feet. "No, stop it. Leave me alone."

I light a second candle, and place it on my desk in the far corner. The light spills across the room, and the shadow vanishes.

I feel a little better. She can't, after all, come from the shadows if there are none around me. Light, then, is all I need. I open the top drawer of my dresser. I have six more candles there, in various states of use: some are mere stubs. Extravagant, but

Citizeness Michelet gives me her used ones, after a point. I light them all.

One for my desk. One for the window-sill, to keep out the dark that presses from outside. One on the desk-chair, which I pull out into the centre of the room. One for the dresser. Four, I place at the four corners of my bed, ringing me in as though in a magic circle.

Finally, my room is ablaze: not quite literally, although if my landlady were to see it, she would be horrified at the danger of fire. Candles sprinkle the dark corners of the room, their flickering flames casting strange grey ghosts on the ceiling but banishing the deep, dark shadows that I dread. It's oddly beautiful, like being in a crowd of stars. Stars never hurt anybody. They glow cold, bright and remote, far above all of this.

I fall asleep with the light dancing on my closed lids, and the shouts of the crowd are only a whispered memory.

*****

It's that night the dreams start to change. Or, if they are not dreams at all, then something else does.

*****

Sophia greets me at the door as she always does, smiling and ushering me inside.

"I'm so glad you saw my candle in the window," she says as she closes the door behind us. "I thought I might have missed you walking past. My sister isn't here after all. Her friend Eloise – her husband is in prison, and tonight one of her daughters is ill. My sister has gone to help care for the little girl. Only think: she has five children, all under nine, and they make her pay for her husband's upkeep in prison in addition to what they need themselves."

"Her husband was denounced as a traitor," I say. "Why is your sister helping her?"

"Eloise is no traitor," Sophia says. "Nor are her children. Her husband was unfairly accused. He had some sympathy for the dead queen at the time of her execution, it is true, and he made some unwise statements to that effect, but his heart was always with -"

"We have to leave, Sophia," I hear myself say. I don't know I am going to say it. My voice is speaking for me.

Sophia blinks, startled. Her face looks pale in the candlelight; I can see the individual freckles on her nose.

"What do you mean?" she asks. "And go where? Now?"

"Within the week," I say. "I'm not talking about leaving the house. I mean we need to leave Paris. Possibly France altogether, if I can get passage to England. I'll do my utmost. But we cannot stay here."

"I don't see why not," she retorts. "This is my home."

"It's a well of blood," I say, bluntly. "And it grows deeper by the day."

"Rivers of blood have been shed for the gold of Peru," she says, but she doesn't quite meet my eyes as she says it. "Should not liberty have the same right to sacrifice lives?"

I grind my teeth, frustrated. "That's something you've read in one of those papers, or been told. You've seen that contraption at work for yourself. It has a mind of its own. It won't stop until it eats all of France."

"That's ridiculous," she says. "It's a machine, under the control of free, enlightened people. And they are winning us the war."

"I can get us out of Paris," I say. "Next Saturday, perhaps, or Tuesday at the latest. I have a friend who knows these things. Tell me you wouldn't go with me."

Sophia says nothing.

"Sophia," I say. I swallow painfully. "I love you. The hours I've spent with you have been the best of my life – even here, even with all this. I want you to come with me, and I want you to marry me."

Neither my declaration nor my proposal seem to have any effect on her, which stings. She seems to be thinking. It cost me a good deal, to say that to her. She could at least look at me.

"If I were to come," she says, slowly, "could Marie come as well?"

I shake my head. "No," I say. "Two people only. That would be the utmost I could do – I would need all my money to get us out. This man I know needs paying, for one thing."

"I thought you said he was a friend of yours."

I laugh. "Not that much of a friend."

"Well, then," Sophia says, and this time she does look at me. "Of course I cannot go. Leave Paris – France, even – and leave Marie behind? Do you have any idea what would happen to her if word reached the wrong ears that I had fled with you, and they came here to question where I had gone?"

"You couldn't tell her," I say quickly. "She can't be able to give us away."

"She never would," Sophia retorts. She is angry now. "And they'd put her in prison for it. She'd die in there, or be dragged out to be executed one day when it suits them. Do you think I could live with that, or would want to?"

"Do you think I could leave without you?" I snap. I'm angry now too: I, who in my waking life am never angry. Now, I could kill her. I'm embarrassed, and frustrated, and furious with her; it is as if somebody else is feeling it for me. "You're asking me to stay here to die."

"I'm not asking you to do anything!" she snaps back. "I'm telling you what I will not do! If you want to leave the country, then leave. I'll miss you, but that's it. You don't own me, or I you."

"I love you," I burst out. "Don't you understand? I would have left long ago if it weren't for you. I've torn my life apart to stay near you. I've put myself at risk, countless times, coming here to meet you."

"I never asked you to," she says. "And I never said I wanted to marry you."

"Stop it!" I say, and before I can stop myself I'm grabbing her shoulders. She twists out of my grasp, furiously, and my hand curls into a fist and flies at her.

I don't quite hit her: perhaps she moves out of the way, or perhaps I have just enough control left to let the blow go wide at the last moment. But the force of it horrifies me – horrifies her, too, I can see – and I can't stop it. My feelings are something apart from me, or at least my movements are. I'm breathing hard, and there's sweat prickling my brow.

"Get out!" she demands. Her voice has risen almost to a shriek, and I wonder if, maybe, she is afraid of me. I'm afraid of me. The passions that fire my veins when I reach for Sophia are now searing them with rage, and I don't know what I might do. "Get out!"

* * * * *

I wake with her screams ringing in my ears, like the toll of a bell a thousand miles away. I'm no longer in my room, but downstairs, in my workshop. My nightshirt is soaked with sweat, and I'm shivering. I am clutching my hammer tightly. Very tightly; my knuckles are white.

Around me, the shadows whisper.

* * * * *

When I was a very small boy, there was a time when I would walk in my sleep. My family moved to a house in a village near Marseilles: my father wanted to expand his business. I loved that house, with its creaky floorboards and labyrinthine staircase going from basement to attic. It was not real country, but it was surrounded as much by fields and trees as by other buildings, and I remember the feel of prickly grass swishing about my knees as I cut across from the lane to our back door in the summer evenings. I remember dust motes dancing in the broad beams of sunlight in the kitchen, and raindrops chasing each other down the window panes in my bedroom. I don't remember any terror.

And yet, from the first night, something in that house took hold of me. My mother would come downstairs to find me wandering the halls, pale and wide-eyed; I answered her when she spoke, though she would never tell me what I said. Sometimes, if she didn't find me, I would wake up outside, shivering in the morning dew. The doctor told her that I would grow out of it, and to lock me in my room. The following morning, I woke to find my nails torn and bloody, and grooves and scratches on the door where I had clawed at it to escape. I began to grow listless, then feverish.

Finally, my mother took me away. I stayed with an aunt for a month, and then my father's business failed and our family moved back to Paris.

As I said, I don't remember being afraid of any of this. My mother told me most of it, when I was somewhat older and we were talking late at night.

She didn't tell me that ten years later, when she and my father were in Marseilles and I was at school, she had met someone who knew the house. Nor did she tell me that, when the owners after us had taken up the floorboards in my old room, they had found the withered body of a child concealed there. I learned that later, when I went out there after my mother's death to see it for myself. I don't know why she didn't tell me. I don't know what it means.

I don't know what my visits to Sophia mean, either. I don't know how she can visit me in shadows, when she's flesh and blood in my dreams. But I know I've wandered in my sleep before, and that, afterwards, they found a child dead.

* * * * *

I wash and dress as usual, but I continue to feel shivery and exhausted. Citizeness Michelet is a broad-faced, business-like woman who nonetheless possesses a streak of protectiveness toward me. When she brings my breakfast, she tuts disapprovingly.

"You don't look at all well, Citizen," she says. "You're very pale."

"I'm perfectly well," I say to her. "I didn't sleep very much last night."

"You want to take care of yourself," she says. "Things have been exciting lately. You don't want to let it overstretch you."

"It's nothing to do with me," I say.

I hesitate, as she puts a bowl of gruel in front of me.

"Have you ever seen me out of my bed at night?" I ask suddenly. "Perhaps down in the workshop, in my nightgown?"

"Oh, yes, Citizen," Citizeness Michelet says. She seems unsurprised by the question, and she answers it without hesitation. "I hear you moving about your workshop often, at night.

Sometimes I hear your voice. You talk to yourself, sometimes. Mutter."

"But seen me?" I persist, though my heart has sunk. "Have you seen me?"

"Certainly," she says. "A few weeks ago, we spoke. It was when all that noise was going on outside – the celebrations, you know. I hope I'm as loyal a citizen as the next woman, but so late into the night... I came to the kitchen for a drink, to help me sleep. You were there, sitting at the table. We spoke of how strong the light was, from the moon and the fires."

"And?" I say, quickly, seeing her hesitate. "Of what else?"

"I don't remember," she says. I don't quite believe her. "It was very late. I was tired. Nothing of consequence."

"Citizen Michelet," I say, carefully. "I don't remember speaking to you. I don't remember leaving my bed. I think I'm acting in my sleep."

Once again, she reacts without surprise. In fact, she nods, as if satisfied. "I thought as much," she says. "You did not seem at all yourself. You looked very white, and you said things that I knew you could not possibly mean. Things about France, and the Terror. Of course, I didn't tell anybody. You're an excellent citizen, I know that. You've proved that."

She's telling me that she has saved my life, I know. But right now, I don't care. "It doesn't concern you?" I ask. "To hear that you had a conversation with a man talking in his sleep?"

"Concern me, yes," she says. "I told you, when I came in, you're clearly unwell. You need to take care of yourself, or you'll be headed for a nervous collapse. But it certainly doesn't surprise me. You've been under a good deal of strain lately. What with your wife..."

"What does she have to do with this?" I snap. The sudden violence of my anger startles even me, and for the first time Citizeness Michelet blinks and frowns. I'm never angry. Only in my sleep, and only at Sophia. "What business is it of yours what I say or do?"

"Such things are everyone's business in the Republic, Citizen," Citizeness Michelet says. She sounds placating, but she's looking at me strangely. "But of course, I didn't mean to upset you."

"I'm not upset," I insist. My heart is pounding in my ears. It sounds like the thud of a guillotine, coming down again and again.

* * * * *

I just won't sleep, that's all. I tell myself this as the light outside begins to fade, as the crowds outside begin to thin. Whatever is happening, whatever I am doing or about to do, it cannot happen if I refuse to sleep. Whoever I am protecting – Sophia, or myself – they will be safe if I remain awake.

I usually stop work at six o'clock, but this time I keep working as that hour comes and passes. The sunset bathes the pale grey walls and cobblestones and wrought iron balustrades, as golden and dreamy as if there never was a guillotine around the corner. I can hear voices in the street, laughing on their way home or to dine, and it's difficult to believe they were raised in bloodlust such a short time ago.

I just won't sleep. I'll hold the world like this. I won't see Sophia, and I won't sleep.

The light turns grey, and then darkens. I light a candle, and begin sanding down the cabinet that I've been hammering all day. The shop begins to cool in the evening. Citizeness Michelet sticks her head in the door, yawning, and is surprised to see me still there.

"Goodness, I would have thought you'd gone upstairs by now," she says. "It's past eleven."

"I just have some work left to do," I say.

She yawns again. I wish she'd stop. "Well, I'd like to shut up down here, if I may," she says. "How much longer will you be?"

So then I have to go upstairs, into my dark bedroom with its sloping floor. I sit down on the hard bed, and try to ignore the way the shadows make the objects unfamiliar. I would light a candle to banish some of the darkness, but I have none left after last night. Stupid not to have ordered more. I don't feel well: my head is throbbing, and my limbs are aching and weary.

It's quiet out there now. I hear a few scattered footsteps from the streets, once a bark of a laugh. The sound of my own breathing seems very loud.

And then, as I knew it would, that sound begins to change. A mutter first, and then voices, and then a roar. I can hear a thin scream, and a thud. The voices rise in cheers. There's another thud. This time no scream accompanies it. The breeze coming through the window seems to bring with it the scent of blood.

Out of the corner of my eye, on the chair beside my bed, I see the shadows shift. I will not look. I know they are resolving themselves into a shape. A slim, youthful figure, with a wisp of curl down the side of her face. I can feel the heat of her eyes on me.

"What are you?" I ask. "Why won't you leave me alone?"

The shape that is Sophia does not reply. I feel that this time, if I only turned my head, I could see it properly. I don't turn my head.

"I can't help it," I say. "I'm visiting you in my sleep. It's not me who asks you to leave France; I'm speaking in a dream. I don't want to hurt you. I don't want to put you in danger. I never asked for the world to turn into this."

The shouts are getting louder. If I concentrate on them, they'll become names I don't want to hear. They always do. I lie back on the bed and close my eyes against the red glow that seems to be permeating the room without illuminating it.

"Go away," I whisper. I'm so tired. "Just go away."

The thud and the scream press against my head, and inside my head.

* * * * *

As usual, Sophia opens the door herself. She's in her night-dress, with a threadbare robe wrapped around her, and her long curls are hanging loose about her face. She's carrying a candle, and the light from it is the only light in the house. This time, she's not expecting me. Her eyes, a little swollen with sleep, widen and then darken at the sight of me.

"I don't want to talk to you," she says.

"I need to talk to you," I say. She gasps a little as I push past her, driving the edge of the door into her ribs. "Your sister's not here, is she?"

"No," she says. She closes the door behind me and puts the heavy candle-stick on the dresser nearby, but her eyes are furious. I'm not welcome to stay. "No, she's staying with Eloise – the little girl has grown worse. Luckily for you, or you'd be out of here so fast your head would spin. She thinks you're no good, and after yesterday, I'm not sure she's wrong."

"I didn't hurt you," I say.

"That time," she says, folding her arms.

"I'm sorry," I say. I hear my voice drop, cajolingly. "Sophia, I didn't mean what I said. I love you. I want to protect you."

"You want to protect yourself," she counters. "Because you're afraid. You're afraid of the uprisings, and the executions. You're afraid of the Republic. You're afraid that one day there's going to be a knock on the door, and they'll come for you."

"Aren't you?" I demand.

"No!" she retorts. "Why should I be? I'm a citizen of France. This is my revolution."

"You're not that naïve!" I say, frustrated. I feel my hands tense into fists, and try to force them to relax. "It was your revolution, once, perhaps. But the tide is turning. The Girondins are losing power – if they're not arrested themselves by the end of the month, I'll be astonished. When that happens, their supporters will be in danger. That includes you. You must know that."

"Perhaps I am that naïve," Sophia says. It's as if she has heard nothing past that accusation. "Perhaps I choose to be."

"Nobody *chooses* to be naïve," I scoff. "Nobody chooses not to know things."

Sophia actually laughs. I hate the sound of it; I'm deadly serious, and she's laughing at me. It hurts, and I feel my anger flare. "You're naïve yourself, if you think that! Everyone chooses not to know something. We used to choose not to know we were downtrodden and dying, and there was no chance for us. The Revolution came, and woke us all up to it, one by one. We freed ourselves. Now we choose not to know that our Revolution is turning to ashes around us, and that sooner or later, it will probably drown in its own blood. Well, why not? If I am to die in a dream, I'd rather this one than the old one, the one where there was no hope."

"I don't choose not to know," I snap. "I don't choose to die in any dream. I'm getting out of this ridiculous country."

"Oh, yes, you're so clever, aren't you, Monsieur?" Sophia mocks. "You see everything so clearly. Well, I'll tell you some things you choose not to see. You choose not to see that you're a bully, and a bloody fool. You choose not to see that I'm never going to leave my family and my country for you, no matter how much you posture and argue."

"Stop it," I warn. The muscles in my arm twitch.

"Or what?" she challenges. "You'll come at me with your fists again? Oh, yes, I can see that suiting you. That's your way of not knowing, isn't it? Anyone that tells you anything you don't want to hear, you lash out at them like a wild dog that's been poked with a stick."

"Sophia," I say, and hear my voice darken. "Stop it."

"You think I'm afraid of you?" Sophia says. She's not laughing anymore. "My gentleman caller. Look at it out there. My city is falling. Our dreams are dying. You're not important. At any moment, my revolution could come through those doors and drag me to the guillotine. You're *nothing*. What do you honestly think you could do to me?"

I feel rage – true, hot rage – and I feel it flood out of my chest and animate my limbs. I feel it, but at the same time it's not what I feel at all: I am apart from myself, watching myself in horror, crying no, no, stop, you'll hurt her. I am seething with anger that is not mine, and that anger snatches up the candlestick from the table. I feel the cool curve of the metal in my fist, and the heat of the candle flame.

"I said *stop it*," I hear myself say, and I hit her.

Right until the second before I bring down the candlestick, she thinks I won't harm her. I can see it in her scornful eyes, in the confident tilt of her chin. The anger in me takes a vicious satisfaction at the moment when her eyes widen, her mouth opens slightly, and she tries, too late to flinch out of the way. The candlestick catches her on the side of her head. She falls.

She lies there on the ground, silent; moving a little, but not much. There's blood starting from her temple. I think she's trying to crawl for the door.

Stop it. I scream the words in my head. Stop it. Stop it.

My body raises the candlestick, and hits her again.

* * * * *

I wake.

* * * * *

I don't get out of bed that morning. I can't go down to my shop, and work. The hammer and the saw won't blot it out this time. I killed her. I knew, somehow, that I would, and yet I couldn't stop myself visiting her. Until last night, I didn't even try: if I had, perhaps I could have managed it somehow.

And yet, why, if I killed her tonight, has her ghost been with me for so long before? What is she, that she can haunt her murderer before her own death?

Outside, I can hear the shouts of the crowd. I burrow down under my covers, press the blankets to my ears, until I am hot and stifled and I can scarcely breathe. It's no use. With the crowds quieter, I can hear the guillotine even more clearly. Its blade comes down over and over again, and I flinch each time under its blow.

There's a knock at the door. I don't move. Citizeness Michelet comes in: I hear the rustle of her skirts.

"Aren't you coming down, Citizen?" she asks. "The shop's empty."

"I'm unwell," I say, without poking my head out from the blankets. "I just want to sleep."

"Shall I call a doctor?"

"Leave me alone," I say. "Please."

There is silence for a while. Then I hear the door quietly close, and know from the feel that she has left the room.

I just want to sleep. There can be no danger in it now. I want an ordinary dream, an endless one, to block out the nightmare.

I feel the shadows move beside the bed. I feel them become another person in the room. I feel her slim body, her hanging curls, the movement of the air as she breathes. I don't open my eyes.

"Jacques," she says. I know the voice. "I'm here."

I don't move. I don't open my eyes.

"I know you're awake," she says. "I always know. Why don't you look at me?"

My heart is thundering in my ears, my limbs are on fire to move, my nerves are screaming to run. I don't move.

"You killed me," she says. "And now you won't even look at me."

* * * * *

I know when the darkness falls, even without opening my eyes. I know because they come for me.

"Jacques," her voice says.

"Leave me alone," I say. "It's not my fault."

I feel the rush of her body pass my bed, and it begins.

I don't open my eyes, not once. But with my eyes closed, I see everything. The things I refused to look at, and the things I did not.

I see a head mounted on a pole, waving its gory hair high above a jeering crowd. I see bodies piled in the streets, and men and women alike mounting them and laughing. I see blood spilling into the gutters. And I hear the screams, and the cheers, mingling into one another until I cannot tell them apart.

I see a woman standing at the guillotine, chin held high, eyes defiant. I see Sophia fall and hit the ground.

"I'm sorry," I say, finally, desperately. I still don't look up. The images playing across my eyes are trapped inside my head, but even to release them, I will not open my eyes. I squeeze them shut even more tightly.

The floor is covered with blood.

* * * * *

The next morning, I wake. The room is quiet and still, and there is sunlight spilling onto the wooden floorboards.

I get out of bed. I should have done it long ago. I haven't eaten all day yesterday, or much the day before; my limbs feel like water and my head is swimming. Still, I wash, and dress, shivering. Inside, beneath it all, I feel oddly calm.

I killed her. It was my fault. I've been hiding from it for too long: far longer than this one day. It's over now.

* * * * *

It's the second time I've seen Sophia's house in daylight. For the first time I can remember, though I must have done it countless times, I raise my fist and knock. After a short time, the door swings open.

I see a slim body, fair hair tied back, Sophia's nose, and for a moment I feel a tiny thrill of hope – very tiny, but it hurts coming to life and it hurts worse when it dies. The woman is older than Sophia; her mouth is wider and her eyes are lighter. There's a resemblance, more than a chance one, but that's all.

"You're not Sophia," I say.

"No," the woman says. She looks surprised. "I'm Marie Abelard. Sophia was my sister."

Was. "She was murdered, wasn't she?" I say. "She was murdered in this house, just inside this door."

"Yes," Marie says. "How did you –?"

"I murdered her," I say. I say it in a rush, before I can change my mind. The relief comes first, then the pain, as though a weight that has been crushing me and yet numbing me has been lifted. I don't know what will happen now. But I've said it. "I didn't mean to. I promise. Last night, when I came to her, I only wanted her to run away with me. To leave France, and escape across the Channel to England. But she wouldn't do it. She didn't want to leave you, and she –"

"Citizen," Marie interrupts. Her face, which had paled in shock at first, is beginning to furrow in confusion. "When did you say this happened?"

"Last night," I say.

Marie shakes her head. "Monsieur, that can't be true. Sophia wasn't killed last night. Sophia was killed six months ago."

* * * * *

It's strange to be inside that house by daylight, that house I know so well by darkness and candlelight. Marie gestures toward the armchair by the fireplace in the front parlour, and when I put my hand on the armrest I feel the hard circle of a cigar burn. I made that myself, one night last week, as I sat smoking by the fire and Sophia spilled into my lap. I stubbed out my cigar, and put my arms around her waist. I can remember the feel and smell of her hair tickling my cheek as she leaned forward to kiss me.

Six months ago. Sophia was killed six months ago.

Marie brings me a glass of wine; cheap wine, in a chipped glass, but it's very welcome. I'm trembling, and I feel sick.

"Drink," she says. "You look as though you're about to faint. Then tell me what you could possibly have meant by coming here and confessing to the murder of my sister."

I lift the glass to my lips. My teeth chatter against the glass, but I force myself to swallow.

Marie sits opposite, and watches. The expectant set of her head does look like Sophia.

"I've been visiting your sister," I say at last. "At night, in my sleep. That is – mostly at night. Sometimes, in the day, she visits me, but that's not..." I draw a breath. "When I close my eyes, I come to this house. She welcomes me. We're lovers."

"You and my sister," Marie says. Her voice is without expression. "Recently, you say?"

"Over the last few weeks," I say. "I don't how I met her, or how she knows me. I didn't know for certain she was real, at first – not until I came here in daylight, and saw the house. I thought I saw her at the window. Perhaps I saw you. Last night, I came to her again. I tried not to, but I couldn't stop myself. I asked her to run away with me, away from France. She refused. And I killed her."

"It wasn't last night," she repeats. "Six months ago, I spent the night with a friend, a woman who lives alone with her daughter. The child was sick; she needed my help. I told Sophia to lock the door and let nobody in. When I came back, I found her lying dead on the floor. I thought later I could smell the blood from the corridor, but the wound on her temple was only small. The candlestick lay beside her. I thought her face looked a little surprised. I knew that whoever had killed her, it was someone she knew, and had let into our house, and had not thought, even as the blow came down upon her head, would really hurt her so badly."

"Then I killed her six months ago," I say. "And she's been haunting me..."

But even as I speak, my mind has pointed out that this makes no sense. Six months ago? I wasn't dreaming six months ago. I wasn't haunted six months ago. Why would I be? Six months ago, I was a whole human being.

"It wasn't you, Monsieur," Marie says. "It couldn't have been. I lived with Sophia. I knew her, and I knew the people she knew. I've never seen you before in my life."

"In my dreams, though, I'm her murderer," I say. "I come to visit her at night. We're lovers."

"Edward," Marie says. She says it with satisfaction, but also with relief. More relief, perhaps, than can be accounted for by the confirmation that she hasn't just given wine to a murderer. "Edward Forester. He was an Englishman living in the city. They had been lovers for a year. She thought he would marry her one day. I believe he did love her, in his way. But he was always jealous. I knew it was him, though he claimed he hadn't been there that night."

"She wouldn't leave you behind," I say. "She refused to run away with him. He became angry with her, and he struck her with a candlestick. She fell." Her words catch up to me. "What do you mean, he *was*?"

"He's dead too," Marie says. "Denounced, and executed two weeks ago. When did your dreams begin, Monsieur?"

"Two weeks ago," I say. I feel sick.

I'm not visiting Sophia every night. And she's not visiting me. It's her murderer. Somehow, all this time, Sophia's murderer has been telling me what happened to her.

"Edward Forester," I repeat. And I feel my actions in my dreams disassociate from me and take the shape of him.

"He was a tall man," Marie says. "Taller than you, and stronger: more handsome too, if you'll forgive me saying. Very attentive, very reserved. But there was always something in his eyes I did not like."

"He came to me," I say.

"Paris is so crowded these days, with the ghosts of the recent dead," Marie says wearily. "It's not surprising that some might come back to lie on the minds of the living."

"My wife died," I say. It's the first time I have ever said the words. They come haltingly, but they won't be held back any longer. "Her name was Eleonore. She was denounced to the people, and killed at the guillotine. I denounced her."

Marie looks at me without surprise.

Elle was twenty when I met her, and I was twenty-two – six years ago, which in these times is an entire lifetime. Regimes rise and fall in less time than that. Kings and Queens die, and ideals turn to ash. We met in her father's shop, as she helped him stock the shelves with tobacco. She collided with me, intent on her work or dreaming of something else. I cannot say why I fell in love with her, only that I did, in the movement of her head towards me and the smile on her face as she begged my pardon. We were married a year later.

She wanted children. I didn't. I couldn't tell her the real reason for this. I couldn't even put it into words for myself.

"The times are so uncertain," I said, instead. "Riots, and deaths. It's not the time to bring up a child."

"All times are uncertain, Jacques!" she'd exclaimed, exasperated. "There's always death. All the more reason to bring life into the world."

And that was the problem. I couldn't imagine a child as life. When I thought of children, I thought of one already dead. Dead, and under the floorboards of a room in a house near Marseilles.

It had been my first ghost, that child. Its father had murdered it, ten years before I was born. It wanted me to tell someone where its body was. But I failed it. I was too young, and I didn't understand. I have no such excuse this time.

I used to argue with her about her support of the revolutionaries. I urged her to stay out of it all: the riots, the colour, the violence, the hope.

"Don't be naïve," I urged her once, as once Edward urged Sophia. "It's nothing to do with us."

"Of course it is," she said. "We're alive. That makes it to do with us."

She was brave, and I have never been so. I think she realised that, as the Bastille fell and the people took power, and then again as the heads began to fall. I thought at the time she had come to hate me for it, but perhaps I had only come to hate myself.

They told me that if I denounced her, I would save myself. They told me that no harm would come to her if she were innocent: she would have a fair trial, and then she would come back to me. They told me that if I did not denounce her, I would not save her, and would be executed myself as a traitor. What person, given that choice, would not willingly join the woman he loved in prison rather than hand her over to the mercy of the guillotine? But I handed her over. I told them what they wanted to hear, and they came for her before I could even return home to warn her. When I ran home, my heart pounding, my limbs trembling, praying for the chance to undo what I had done, the door was shattered and the floor inside trampled by boots. The picture of us that hung above the fireplace had been slashed. I don't know who did that.

She wasn't held for very long; a matter of days. Then the guillotine took her, and she joined the ranks of the dead.

"And so," Marie says, as I finish, "you are a murderer too."

"Yes," I say. "Just like Edward. Maybe that was why he came to me."

We sit in silence for a while.

"Is he sorry?" Marie asks eventually. "Edward. Is he sorry for what he did to my sister?"

"Yes," I say. I didn't realise I knew it. I had been feeling his guilt for a long time, but I had taken it for my own. "Yes, he's very sorry. He's sorry he did it, and he's sorry he never told you. He wanted you to know."

Marie nods. "Then I'm sorry too."

We sit a while longer, but neither of us have anything more to say to the other. The house seems shadowed with memories. After I finish the glass in my hand, I say my farewells, and Marie nods and walks me to the street.

She is about to close the door behind me, when she stops. I stop too. "It was I who denounced Edward," she says. "I went to the Selection Committee, and I told them he had been selling Royalist pamphlets from his wine shop. It wasn't true, of course. But he was a foreigner, and they believed me. They didn't believe me when I told them he had killed Sophia, but they believed that. They threw him in the Conciergerie for three months, and then they took him to the guillotine. I watched as his head tumbled from his shoulders, and the blood spurted from his neck. So you see, when I said you were a murderer too, it wasn't Edward of whom I was thinking."

I say nothing.

"If you see Sophia," Maria says, "tell her I will be joining her very soon."

* * * * *

I walk back to my shop, through the streets that right now are lazy and quiet. A light drizzle darkens the paving stones, and cloaks the road ahead in mist. I walk through the Place de la Revolution, for the first time in many months. The guillotine stands silent in the square, and the rain cloaks it too.

Citizeness Michelet lets me through the side-door, scolding me for letting myself get so wet when I've been so unwell. I thank her, take off my cloak, and go into the work-room, where the shadows wait.

They're but shadows, at first. I knew they would be. I stand there, my shoes still dripping water, and wait.

Out of the corner of my eye, the darkness shifts, and resolves itself into a shape. Her shape.

"You killed me," she said yesterday. "And now you won't even look at me."

I never looked at her as I killed her, either. I stayed in my shop and hammered and sawed and rasped, as she was loaded into a cart with her long curls cut. I stayed there as she was taken down the long road to the Place de la Revolution, as they pulled her roughly from the cart and led her to the scaffolding. It was a cold, grey day. I don't know what she saw or thought as she stood and waited, if she said anything as they placed her head in the guillotine. I heard the thud and the cheers from where I bent over my work, and I never looked up.

I look at her now. The slim body, the wide dark eyes, the small upturned nose.

It's not Sophia Abelard. It never has been. It's my wife.

"I'm sorry, Elle," I say to her. "I'm sorry that I never gave you a child. I'm sorry that I killed you."

Eleonore watches silently. I don't think she forgives me. I didn't expect her to. Not yet.

I will dream of her death tonight, and I will not look away.

I go to work, as I live, in the company of the dead.

Vacancy
Hamish Crawford

"I suppose you want to know why I did it. Not that I did, but you've probably made up your mind."

There wasn't any point trying to beat around the bush. I was cornered. They'd caught up with me, and I was sitting in an uncomfortable folding metal chair in an interrogation room so dark I could hardly make out my audience. It didn't help that my interrogator wore such a drab jacket, and that he kept on his black gloves. I guess he didn't want to touch the crazy in case any of it rubbed off.

"I've got a lot of reasons," I said. "Every day ... every day I feel ground down by my life, by the world. Maybe my job makes me sick, maybe my choices make me sick. Other people definitely make me sick. I can't say I ever enjoyed working and sometimes I feel I'm watching some other guy walk around, and I want to stop him doing stupid things but I have no control over him. I hate it when you're driving along and you don't see someone and they think you're cutting them off and they give you the finger. Why do they always assume the worst about you?"

He didn't answer.

"Maybe it's the world," I continued. "Maybe I woke up one morning and heard one news broadcast too many and from there-"

"Why don't you just tell me how it all started?" he asked.

"How it started ..."

It really started with a roommate. I was thirty-six and single, and I didn't need the money, I just needed some company.

I'd never shared a place with anyone and it seemed selfish to have a two-bedroom apartment downtown, with property costing what it did. So, I put an ad in the paper and a few people answered it. But as soon as I met this one guy, I knew he was the right roommate for me. He didn't just ask the boring questions, so I knew we'd have some interesting conversations.

"Big place—how come the rent's so low, Daniel?" I also liked that he called me by my first name a lot. I felt like I was his friend already.

"I don't need the money. I ... hope this doesn't sound weird, but I'm a bit tired of being by myself. I wouldn't mind a friend to talk to."

"That doesn't sound weird at all. One human being reaching out to another, two total strangers, who just want to share their common humanity with each other. Why should a simple act of society be weird, Daniel?"

I was actually a little touched by this efficient yet sentimental assessment. Yes! It was exactly what I was thinking but I couldn't put it into words. Why couldn't two strangers just connect? Why were we all so afraid? I shook his hand and he agreed to move in.

He showed up the following week. He didn't have many possessions. He had a lot of books, but only a single battered valise. I wasn't surprised because when he arrived with his stuff he was wearing the same suit he wore when we first met. It was well made but a little worn, in a faded shade of brown and with a double-breasted jacket.

The first couple of weeks were a little odd. He rarely came out of his room. I'd bought a new popcorn maker and I was looking forward to sharing some with him.

"No thanks, Daniel," he said immediately. I hadn't even asked him anything. It was kind of rude. "Sorry, but I'm a little tired today. Thanks anyway."

Since he had conducted the entire conversation himself, I had nothing to add, so I just mumbled "Maybe another time?" He gave me a non-committal shrug and closed the door. I wouldn't mind, but I had made a lot of popcorn. I put truffle oil in it like lifestyle magazines suggested. I was eating popcorn by myself for a while after that—I think I ended up skipping a couple of dinners on account of it. Let me tell you, I don't think I'll ever put truffle oil on anything again!

So that week passed, then another, then another. The only conversation we had in those early days took place one Saturday. I had no plans so I decided I'd just hang out at a bar across the street. I'd be one of those interesting people who props up the last stool at the end, nursing a glass of beer and reading a book. It always takes a bit of time to motivate myself to go out, especially when I'm not meeting anyone. Tonight my roommate had ventured out of his room and was on the couch, flipping channels. Digital cable has really made channel flipping much less enjoyable hasn't it? You just read the description instead of seeing the show and trying to guess what it's about. I miss those days.

Sorry. Anyway, I asked him, "You know, it occurs to me that you've not had a housewarming party. A moving-in party? I thought you might want to have some friends over and a few drinks. I'd be happy to co-host."

He looked over at me, and his dark eyebrows met in the middle of his forehead in confusion. "Oh, that's very nice of you, Daniel. But I don't really have any friends. I think you're my only friend."

I felt sad for him. I had my jacket half-on, and had really just gotten in the zone for a heavy evening of half-distracted reading and concentrated drinking; but I couldn't rightly leave a man at home with second-rate digital cable right after he told me I was his only friend.

"Hey man, sometimes I feel that way too. But you probably find you have friends—they're just busy on dates or bowling or whatever on Saturdays, so it's hard—"

"Oh Daniel!" he said. "You do go on sometimes. Why don't you go out and have fun? Don't feel bad about me; I'm quite looking forward to a night in. You have to take pleasure in the quiet, peaceful moments. Otherwise so much of life would be ..." He trailed off with a wave of his hand, and he cast his gaze down to the book poking from my jacket pocket. "Jackie Collins, eh? It's nice to have some down-to-earth fun reading every so often. You enjoy it."

I had a reasonably good time that night. I had some really great local ales and excellent sea-bass. What's wrong with being alone, I asked myself? I was able to do anything, didn't have to okay it with anyone, or have anyone say it was a boring night and we should try something new ... sure, sometimes I wish my friends weren't always so busy, but there were a few birthdays coming up and I'd see them then.

There was one thing that kind of spoiled the night. A few tenants in my building had been talking about missing people. I guess a lot—no, they exaggerated, over the last three months it was three or four—people had gone missing and it had all been within a few blocks of the Montana Apartments. "It's not the kind of thing one imagines happening at the Montana," Mrs. Vixis opined, pausing haughtily before the word 'Montana', as though our fancy building was some kind of consecrated ground.

On this particular night, on my way home, I saw a 'Missing Person' paper stuck to the lamppost out front, and it was a young woman from work. I always thought her name was Megan, but 'Serena Gulbis' was what it said on the paper. I wished I had properly talked to her, but I always thought she'd have no time for someone like me. If only she had, though, she wouldn't have gone missing.

I know this sounds awful, but I ended up getting mightily sick of hearing about Serena Gulbis. For weeks after, everyone at work would ask if there had been any word, say what a tragedy it was, wonder how her boyfriend and her family were coping with it. The first few days, I was just as sad as everyone. Sadder, even—somehow the proximity to my building made me feel like I should have seen her, should have been around to help her when it happened.

Crazy, right? You can walk the same streets as your dearest friends and never run into them. I shouldn't feel bad, I told myself.

Part of the sadness was that a lot of people thought she'd turn up sooner or later. I just knew that would never happen. My natural pessimism in action, I suppose. In some ways, that made it more hopeless—the conversations would start, "Has anyone heard any news about Serena?" and the inevitable answer would be a sad, silent shake of the head.

I never volunteered the information that she had gone missing so close to my apartment. Somehow, though, people seemed to know anyway. There was that one asshole who said, "I don't suppose you'd know anything about it, eh Dan?"

"M-me?" I stammered. "What would I know about it?"

"You tell me. Our very own Norman Bates, and no one ever knew ..."

"You think I—? How could you possibly think I was capable...?"

"Why not?"

"I ... I swear ... I couldn't even believe that it happened, that I didn't see anything, didn't have the first clue there was anything ... horrible like that ... happening right under my nose ..." I felt dizzy, and the words that came out of my mouth echoed emptily in my head.

I really hoped that would be the end of it. But that insufferable cretin kept pushing it. He was half-joking, but there in his eyes I saw a glint of curiosity, a morbid fascination to see if I would break down, and if I did, what I might reveal. There was something almost tribal in it, and for all their concerned expressions, my co-workers just stood by and watched. They were just as curious to see this chimp snap.

"Well, how do we know what you're capable of?" he asked. "Any of us? We barely see each other outside the office, for all we know ..."

I still don't really know why I took this so personally. My head spun, and I looked around desperately from one person to the next. I kept trying to calm myself down. He was always making jokes like that, and most people shrugged them off and ignored him.

This time, possibly because of my extreme reaction, everyone around him recoiled in horror. "How could you?" Harriet asked.

"Too soon?" he stammered, trying to play it off casually.

"God, even you should have drawn the line. Daniel's as upset about this as any of us. He doesn't know anything about it, and you can see he's wrenched up inside about it happening so near to him."

I nodded. "Of—of course," I mumbled. "I just ... don't know what to say about it. Poor Megan—I mean, Serena, I just always thought she looked like a Megan. Never even got a chance to talk to her …"

I think I must have been swaying back and forth, because the entire room felt like a listing ship. The two people nearest to me patted my shoulder. The sudden contact stung, and my skin felt sore and tender all over. A wave of nausea overcame me, and I ran to the bathroom.

After that incident, I felt even worse, because everyone started siphoning off their sympathy for Serena to me. "Look how it affected poor Daniel," a couple of people said. I didn't deserve their sympathy, but the most I could do was protest weakly that I was all right.

After week upon week going by with no news, the conversation was brought up and resolved with a few slow, sympathetic nods—nods I matched. Oh, those days were filled with that slow nodding. I guess people do that when they have nothing to say but want to look like they're thinking, reflecting, on the terrible tragedy.

Still, I suppose having nothing to say was better than those idiots who'd start mouthing off about crime and law enforcement. I should have known a disappearance close to home would bring out a lot of prejudices, but boy did I hear more than my fair share of pet theories on who should be blamed and who should be taken off the streets as a result of them. The problem was that, as another guy at work pointed out, that part around the Montana was one of the least threatening neighbourhoods in the city. It was incredibly middle-class, and really, I had walked up and down it at all hours of the night never even feeling like I would get mugged, never mind kidnapped or murdered.

Anyway, these conversations went around and around, poisonously bringing out worse and worse fixations in our staff. Once this became routine, I became a little jaded about it all, and I decided to respond to it with slow and sympathetic nods of my own.

Funnily enough, though I was upset about all this and it really started to prey on my mind, I never once mentioned it to my roommate. I tried to avoid talking about work anyway—it was so deadly dull that it was hard enough to sit through every day, never mind share with another poor soul. Maybe I was also a little concerned that it might prompt him to move out. We didn't spend a lot of time together, but somehow, just having him there with me was a little nugget of stability.

So, the first time I saw my roommate's book was a good month and a bit after he moved in. He had slowly gotten more sociable, and it was nice to have some beers after work and watch the occasional basketball game. I don't know what he did for a living, but I was glad he had such short hours—he always saw me off in the morning and was there when I got back.

It was a beautiful old book. I used to go to second hand bookstores nearly every weekend after I moved to the city. My favourite one was called MacLeod's Books. I always felt there was something magical about old books, old ideas. I was glad to meet finally someone who felt the same way.

I told him this when I saw this dusty old thing that collected all the issues of some magazine called *Nineteenth Century*. He was flipping through it when the basketball was at half time. I mean, *Nineteenth Century*, I thought; how antique can you get? The article he was reading was by 'Mme. E. de Laszowska Gerard'—not exactly Anthony Bourdain!

I was truly enthralled by what Mme. Gerard was writing about. "Look at this, the story of the Scholomance. What a beautiful sounding old word that is." I idly turned a few pages. "What is it, magic?"

"I bet you think that's a load of bollocks, eh Daniel?"

"Not at all," I said politely. I did kind of think magic and astrology and all that was a load of bollocks. But, I'm sure he thought following sports to the extent that I did was kind of silly too.

"No, don't just say that, you should," he pressed. "I'd think it was bollocks too, but, you see, I don't just read this … I believe it, Daniel. I've seen enough to make me believe it's all true, every word of it. Take the Scholomance: an academy deep in the world's oldest mountains where ten evil scholars are taught the lessons of diabolism by the Devil himself."

"Well, why not? Seems reasonable …" I rambled. This conversation was getting odder and odder.

"More than that, even," he continued. "I don't just believe it exists. I think sometimes … I've been there."

I smirked, then spent a moment worried that I'd offended him. But then he snorted with laughter and we laughed and drank and enjoyed the rest of our evening.

* * * * *

I was sufficiently intrigued about the Scholomance to read up on it myself in my spare time. I saw why he found it so interesting. This place, this site of ancient evil somewhere in the mountains, I thought about it a lot. I had recently become pinned to my sterile and empty apartment and my sterile and empty office. All of them were slick and modern, but nowhere felt like a home; nowhere felt like it had history or community in it. It seems odd to think that a kind of 'Satan University' could feel communal, but maybe it was the folklore that it sprang from, Transylvanian and Hungarian and Romanian superstitions. I saw these were warm places, where locals huddled together with their loved ones and told each other fearful stories as the nights grew longer.

One Sunday, I ran into some married friends of mine, Shemina and Josh. I gave them a friendly greeting, but they seemed very concerned. They looked at me like I had risen from the dead.

"Is everything okay Daniel?" Shemina asked.

"Sure, why, what's the problem? I know it's been a while."

"Well, we haven't seen you in so long. And then you said you'd be at Jenna's birthday and you never showed up, and we called and called you."

"Oh ... was that last night? Yeah, I went out with my roommate. We went to a wine bar, had a bit too much to drink. I completely forgot—actually, that's not the only thing I forgot, I blacked out about ten! How embarrassing. Thank God he doesn't drink, or I'd never have gotten home. Sorry about that."

"But you didn't answer your phone?" she asked. I was getting annoyed at her maternal tone.

"Oh, I ... this will sound funny but I lost my phone ages ago. I kind of forgot about it. Didn't seem like there was anyone I called very much." They looked away guiltily as I said this, even though I wasn't meaning to admonish them. It was simply the truth. "Sorry again for causing any concern."

"That's okay Daniel," Josh said, casting a warning glance at his wife. "I told you." He looked back at me and prodded Shemina's elbow. "She was worried, because of all the missing people around your building."

"Oh, yeah. That's so weird, isn't it? I haven't seen anything suspicious. I'm sure I'll be telling that to the police soon enough, because I think another one went missing."

"They think it's every full moon," she said. "Take good care of yourself, Daniel." She grabbed my hand. I flinched at the sudden, unbidden intimacy. "Let's get together soon. You look a bit peaky."

"Working too hard," I explained.

It hadn't felt like I was working too hard, but work was undoubtedly getting worse. I was the first to take responsibility for the decline, which I thought would defuse the tension but didn't. To me, this was a low-level finance position, not my dream career. My boss, Lemy Nattaman, whose pasty face and glum demeanour were legendary around the office, knew too well about my indifference, and somehow revelled in causing me misery. He had heard about my reaction to the Serena Gulbis stuff, and as far as I could tell, my recent vulnerability had only increased his antipathy to me. I'm not a guy who handles confrontation well, so my reaction was to avoid him as much as possible.

One day, though, he called me in for a meeting. I knew from the way things had been going he wasn't going to ask me if I'd prefer a French press for the break-room coffee.

"Daniel, how have things been going?"

I admit, just having him ask that question, as he eased his way behind his pine-scented desk, instantly raised my hackles. I didn't want him to know how things were going. I shrugged and said, "Not too bad."

He repeated my answer back to himself, as if he had never heard the phrase 'Not too bad' before. He said it several times, and then tapped his knuckles against a binder on his desk. "And as for work—"

"Well, it's going. Within reason."

Lemy shrugged and flipped open the binder. "I've been going over staff payroll—just checking your numbers. No need to read anything sinister into it."

"You're the boss. You're entitled to do whatever you want."

Those words came out far more petulantly than I'd intended. Lemy leaned forward, his fingers steepled. Even sitting down, he had a good foot of height on me. I was oddly calm, though, and leaned forward in turn.

"Well, maybe I should come right to the point. There seems to be ... a bit of missing cash."

I frowned. "How much?"

"A lot. Take a look at the zeroes after that number there." He tapped the paper emphatically.

I looked down at the numbers, and involuntarily flinched at the sight of it. It was big all right—nearly ninety thousand dollars.

"Do you mind if I check your numbers?" I flashed a simpering smile and added, "No need to read anything sinister into it." I was probably unwise to say that, but the whole meeting wasn't fazing me. Let's see what this clown can throw at me, I thought. Let's see the worst he's got.

He blinked, then nodded, and shoved the binder across the desk to me. I pulled out a pencil and began adding. I refused his offer of a calculator.

As I worked, I became strangely chatty. "It's refreshing doing some addition by hand. We spend so much time plugging numbers into spreadsheets, don't we? All the amazing skills I've picked up over the years, and it's my skill at typing numbers into a programmed cell that determines where I work, how much I get paid ... does that seem fair?" Probably surprised at the rant, Nattaman sat silently and stared back at me. "Well, Mr. Nattaman, does it seem fair?"

"...I don't want to talk about that, I'd really just like to—"

"It *doesn't*!" I snapped, slamming my fist down on the table. "Does it, Mister Nattaman?"

I was sure this outburst would get me fired, but he replied calmly, "Maybe not for you."

"Maybe not for *me*? What kind of answer is that? Maybe not for anyone! And look!" I slid the binder back his way. "You put these dividends in the wrong column. That's probably why you made your mistake."

He stared back at me for a second. I couldn't help but smile thinly, seeing every potential response flicker across his face: should he reprimand me himself, call security maybe, or just kick me out of his office and go over my head? No farther ahead, he blinked again and looked back down at the calculations.

We both sat silently while he pored over the calculations again. The only sound was the squeak of my chair. I squeaked it repeatedly and purposefully. I was enjoying this sudden rush of power. It might sound petty, but I had a lot of frustrations built up and I was getting a hell of a thrill releasing them this way. For his part, Nattaman paused from his work only to cast me furtive, toxic glances.

Finally, he slid the binder back my way. "I don't think you're right, Daniel. I've done it the way you did it, and it's still showing that discrepancy."

Therefore, I went back and added the numbers up again. Somehow, we kept doing the exact same sums, but I kept coming up with the right number, and Nattaman kept coming up with this $90,000 discrepancy. All in all, we were in there for another hour and a quarter.

Finally, Nattaman shut the binder. "This isn't getting us anywhere. Whether you're aware of it or not, this is your problem. Either you ... sort it out, or I will have to refer it upwards."

"Sort it out? How am I supposed to do that? I've told you and shown you what the problem is." I paused, let the room simmer in the hostility I was radiating out, and then I went in for the kill. "Are you accusing me of embezzling this money?"

Nattaman raised his hands and leaned back in his chair. "Certainly not ... but how would this look to the people upstairs? All I'm saying is ... look, Daniel, if it's returned, no one even needs to know we had this conversation. That's pretty generous."

I stood up and turned away from him. Somehow, this gave me still more power, and I became even angrier as I spoke. "Could I make an alternative suggestion? Two actually. One: you are simply a shoddy mathematician who doesn't want a junior employee to show him up at elementary arithmetic. Two: you have embezzled the money yourself and are taking the opportunity to heap blame onto an employee you think could be an easy scapegoat."

"Why would I think—"

"Oh, don't be so obtuse, sir! I can see you think there's something wrong with me. The way you're talking to me now—you *want* this to be the reason for the oddity, the strangeness of my existence in this workplace, because it explains why someone like me can be so unsatisfied in a position you think is the best he can do with his life. That would make your world a much more secure place. Rather than the truth, which is that I am casually better than you at something you care *far more deeply about*."

These strange, angry words hung in the air. I had no idea I felt this way about any of this, until I said it. Having said it, though, I felt liberated. I didn't want to take back or apologize for anything I had said. Nattaman was leaning right back, as though the blast of my ranting was pinning him against his office wall.

"I understand you have been … affected by events in the office. But this is totally unacceptable."

I chuckled bitterly. "If that's the best you can do, take your numbers to the upstairs people. I'll enjoy showing them what a fool you are." I stormed out of the office, not even bothering to listen to his threats. I noted, with some satisfaction, that the employees were staring at him, rather than me, as I marched back to my desk. I grabbed my coat and went straight home.

When I got back home, though, I thought about what I had done and said. I became less sure of how right I was, and wanted to go back over those numbers again. Most of all, I considered what would happen after he inevitably played his hand to his boss. Though I was utterly convinced he was behind this, he was right that no one would take my word over his.

That night, things got a bit heavy. Thank God my roommate was there, because if I was alone I don't know what I'd have done. I told him about what happened, and how truly odd my reaction was.

"I mean, it was literally like I was possessed. It was … beyond a psychotic episode, it was true id manifesting itself. After all, I don't really have any reason to feel bad about my life, but I do. And that was every frustration I've ever felt about the day-to-day, the walking in to the office, the sitting in the office, the punch-punch-punch of that stupid clock we're all on … sometimes that routine, that mundane and dull routine just makes me want to scream. I know you're thinking, typical first-world problems, much wants more. I mean, don't get me wrong, I'm happy with my money and even though it wasn't the job I dreamed of doing, the word on the grapevine was that I could be looking at a promotion at the end of October."

So I started spilling all this—and more—and feeling just as stupid telling him as right now, telling you. I had put on a Ramones album, because that always cheered me up when I got feeling like this.

He sat there, and he listened, and at the end of it all, he nodded. It was just a simple, straightforward nod, but I instantly felt a wave of relief.

"Well, you clearly needed to say what you said. Why do you think you felt so resentful? Not that I'm saying it was unwarranted. In fact, it sounds like Nattaman had it coming."

"It just brought home every ... every frustration I've had behind that desk," I said. "I just thought of something that happened a while ago. There was one day I had to go down to the mailroom. The lady was sorting through my letters and was in the middle of telling her co-worker some story, right? So there they were, and they were laughing uncontrollably. Like, she laughed so hard she had to put all my letters down, apologize, and start all over again. And you always feel like a schmuck when people are laughing and you didn't hear the joke. So I asked her, 'What's so funny?'

"She looked at me and said, 'Oh, it's just something a friend of ours did.'

"'What?' I pressed. I needed a laugh that day, so I began looking forward to sharing this little glimpse of a character outside my sphere.

"Then she gets all snooty with me. 'God, you upstairs types are all the same. Can't we just have our own thing? You have to muscle in and steal our lives. Isn't it enough that you get to boss us around and make things miserable for us every day?'

"I took my mail and headed back upstairs. When I got to the elevator, I heard her laughing again. She had to hoard her goodwill; she couldn't reach out and share some with someone who needed it? I mean, I wasn't trying to muscle in on anything, I just wanted to know someone else's story, press my face against the glass and look in on another life…"

He looked at me, and ran a hand through his fiery ginger hair. The beer had flushed his cheeks, and for the first time I noticed that his eyebrows were a different colour, a very dark brown. So odd was the mismatch that I wondered if he dyed his hair.

"Was that Serena Gulbis?" he asked.

"It was," I nodded, the unpleasant memory of the 'Missing Person' poster, and all that ongoing workplace misery, returning to my mind. "How did you know her?"

"Oh, I saw that paper downstairs," he said brusquely.

"Of course." I wasn't sure why I was so suspicious just then. "Actually, I'd forgotten all about that day until I saw that poster. It was the only time I ever spoke to her."

"They never did find her. I imagine they've closed the book on her by now."

"Horrible, isn't it?"

"Oh, I don't know." He must have seen the look I gave him, because he quickly added, "Oh don't get me wrong. It's horrible all right. But I mean, people are horrible. Aren't they? Fundamentally. You know that better than anyone, don't you Daniel? Look at what you did."

I suddenly felt my heart beating heavily. What was he getting at? Was he accusing me of something? "What … what did I do?" I asked him.

"You know, renting out a room just so you could have some company."

I laughed, a weight of tension lifted from me. "Oh, *that*. God, I'm sorry, man. I thought you were accusing me of, of …"

"Murdering them? You, Daniel, *murdering* six people?"

"I thought it was five."

"Nah, some guy vanished last week. It's the families I feel bad for."

Thankfully, our pizza arrived, and we changed the subject to my ex-girlfriend. That always got some laughs.

It was only when I got off an elevator one Saturday that I realized what Mrs. Vixis had been saying. A group of her friends all huddled in the lobby, ready to go to Sunday brunch or some old-person thing that until that moment I found enviously charming. They looked at me in unison and, I swear to God, a shiver ran down my spine. It was only as I walked out the front that I heard her say, "He thinks he's fooling everyone. Played dumb when I talked to him."

God, I felt faint when I heard that. I knew exactly what she meant, as the last time we'd talked was about the missing people, when she paused before saying 'Montana'. Somehow, she'd gotten it into her head that I knew something about the missing people. That I was kidnapping them? The thought of it made me weak, I tell you.

I was beginning to think it was 'Hate on Daniel Lethem Month' or something. As if it wasn't bad enough dealing with Mrs. Vixis, the situation with Mr. Nattaman kept worsening. I might have guessed most people would take his word over mine, but then I got a memo saying that I caused him emotional harm and was 'abusive in the workplace'. Isn't that workplaces all over, I thought. Years of passive-aggressive morality crushing are impossible to prove or prevent, but as soon as you raise your voice, they get to crucify you.

It didn't help that the payroll error refused to go away. No one could actually find out what I'd done wrong, and I kept adding it up without any money missing, but still they wouldn't believe me.

So it had come to this: a meeting with Nattaman, first thing in the morning. This time he didn't even waste time with pleasantries. As soon as I walked in the door, he stated, "Listen, I've done everything I can, but we can't get past this. We've passed the point where admitting wrong-doing would be helpful."

"Wrong-doing? You're still sticking with that old saw?"

Nattaman laced his fingers and held the resulting heaped hands up to his nose, and breathed in and out in affected contemplation. "Daniel," he said as soothingly as he could muster, "I don't want this to go the same way as last time …" He paused, and looked me up and down as if he had never seen me before in his life. "Jesus, Daniel. Have you seen yourself?"

"What is it?"

"You look awful."

I flashed him a humourless smile. "Yeah, people have been telling me that."

"But I mean … really, have you looked in the mirror recently? You look like you haven't shaved in weeks. That shirt's yellow. And you haven't done up your top button. How many times have we told you about that top button? You've gotta look professional, even if you don't give a damn about this place. And your tie's all crooked; I can see the back of it poking out."

I looked down, and put my hand up to my face. "It hadn't occurred to me," I said, a little surprised to think about it. I actually hadn't realized that several weeks of beard growth had accumulated on my face. This led me to an even stranger realization. "You know, I don't think I've looked at myself in the mirror for a while."

Nattaman rolled his eyes. "Daniel, come on. Be serious with me."

I thought about it to myself. "No, I'm serious. I never look at my face. I don't think I've got any mirrors in the house anymore. I hadn't really noticed it … I'm no oil painting, so maybe it was subconscious."

Nattaman leaned back in his chair. I couldn't believe it, but he seemed almost sincere as he said, "You know, I'm not. We've noticed your behaviour recently, Daniel. Your outburst to me was only the most public manifestation. I've asked your colleagues and they back me up."

"Manifestation?"

"Of some … deep emotional problems. Now, I know everyone was hit pretty hard by what happened to Serena. And I understand there have been other disappearances near where you live. Is that right?"

I nodded, silently. I didn't want to talk about this.

"Now, as horrible as that was and is for you, we really can't have it interfere with the workplace. Check your problems at the door and get on with what needs to be done, eh?"

I wasn't mad at Nattaman any longer. I was somewhat relieved, in fact. So it was pure curiosity in my mind when I asked, "Why are you giving me this advice, Mr. Nattaman? Isn't it a bit pointless when you're just going to fire me?"

"Fire you ..." Nattaman ran a hand through his hair, his eyes wide. He looked as though he hadn't considered that before. "That is one option. Please understand that it isn't what I want. Your work is good enough, though, and we'd be sad to see you leave ..."

"I know. It seems like the only option."

"Of course it isn't the only option, Daniel. And you shouldn't think of this as a door closing ... you'll have more opportunities, I'm sure."

"Thank you for saying that. I'm not sure I agree." I stood up, even though Nattaman started barking that we hadn't actually resolved anything. I reached across the desk, grabbed his hand, and shook it. Then I left the office.

The rest of that day passed in the same surreal glow. I sat at my desk; there didn't seem to be any point in doing anything, so I just sat there staring at my computer, turning over that conversation in my head, repeatedly, obsessively. Had I been paying attention to the world around me, I might have noticed that Nattaman hadn't left his office since his meeting with me.

At around three in the afternoon, something odd happened and I was so out of it I didn't even think about it. I saw my roommate come into the building. He crept along the perimeter of the office floor and entered Nattaman's office. No one seemed to notice him or even look up as he walked in—which was odd, because Nattaman was well known to get hysterical if anyone popped in on him.

So he was in there, and then about ten minutes later, the door opened again and my roommate left. He must have seen me but he didn't say anything, or even acknowledge my presence. He just calmly crept back to the elevator—again; creeping along the walls as if he thought no one would see him—and was gone. The only sign he had even been there was that Nattaman's door was now ajar—again, oddly, since he complained loudly about the noise from the cubicles interfering with his workflow.

Maybe it was my OCD in action, but that open door bugged me. I got up and went over to it. Oh, how I wish I'd just packed it in and headed home, but my curiosity got the better of me, and I peeked into the office.

Nattaman lay sprawled out across the desk, his eyes bulging from their sockets in a near-comic tableau of terror. His neck was swollen, and his entire face was flushed. Now that I thought back on it, he did have a weak heart. That asshole who'd given me the hard time about Serena nearly sent him to hospital after one April Fool.

I went closer to him, and reached out and touched his skin. He was dead ... very dead. I looked behind me, and I frantically considered my options. It was clear that I should have done what they do in movies; rushed out to his secretary and snapped, "Someone call an ambulance! Something terrible's happened!"

Then I thought for a moment. No one had seen my roommate come in. Therefore, to everyone else's eyes I had gone in to see Nattaman, and then the next thing they see is Nattaman dead, with me standing over the body. Why had my roommate visited? What had he done? If it was an accident, why did he leave so calmly, as if nothing had happened? And if it was ...

No. No, my roommate was not a murderer. I, on the other hand, couldn't be cleared of some payroll fraud, so people could quite clearly believe I could be one.

With all these thoughts, I didn't do the movie option. Instead, I sidled my way out of the office, and crept out of the building. And then ran, as fast as I could, home.

By the time Inspector Rimbaud came to visit me, I had become a pariah in the building. They'd close the elevator before I got there, and if I got in with them, they'd step out.

My roommate was horrified to hear about it all. "Huh, it just shows you how people are, doesn't it Daniel, old buddy? You are the nicest person in this whole building. Don't forget that. They hear some scurrilous rumour and they all turn on you. No more dignified than a pack of wild animals... with a lot of cash."

Hearing him say that made me feel a lot better about everything that was happening in my life. Who cared what these pinheads thought of me anyway? I didn't recall having a proper conversation with any of them, so frankly I wasn't missing much in the way of company. And it meant I got to take the stairs, which meant I was losing weight.

When Rimbaud came round, I felt a sinking feeling. Strangely, no one had followed me up about Nattaman's death.

Assuming I was pretty much done there anyway, I stayed home the rest of the week. And I decided not to ask my roommate about visiting the office that day. Damn it, he was the only guy who showed me a shred of goodwill, so it was the least I could do to give him the benefit of the doubt.

However, there we were, with the portly inspector looming over me. I played it as cool as I could, even though I was instantly a little on edge. "What is this about, Inspector?"

"Well, it's about those murders in this area. We're hoping you can help us with our inquiries."

Completely inappropriate though it was, I was so relieved that it wasn't about Nattaman that I burst out laughing. He looked at me with as much official contempt as he could muster, and I apologized. "It's just, you have to understand … I was joking about this to some friends of mine."

"Joking? About murders?" he asked.

"No … God no, the disappearing people turn my stomach. No, just that I really haven't seen anything, but it must be happening close by." I paused, and swallowed. Crossing to the counter to pour myself a glass of water as casually as I could manage, I cleared my throat and asked, "How … how do you know they're murders?"

"Some bones were discovered in the alley outside this building. Human bones. Horrible, to just throw someone away like that, after killing them for some vile ritual."

"Ritual?"

"We think it's the work of a deranged cult," Rimbaud said, putting full venom into the word 'cult'. "People can believe whatever hocus-pocus they like, but when they think it gives them the right to do this … then I've got a problem."

I suddenly thought of that peculiar Scholomance book, and my roommate's *Nineteenth Century* collection. I nervously considered what Rimbaud would make of what until now seemed a quaint tale of bogeymen. I nodded, rapidly. "I totally agree, Inspector."

"You seem nervous, Mr. Lethem."

"Call me Daniel. No, no, not nervous. I'm just … talking about this unsettles me. I always feel unsettled when I think there's something going on that I don't know about. I think it took root in a childhood game of hide and seek…"

"You like to explain yourself a lot, don't you Daniel?" he interrupted.

"People find me a bit strange sometimes."

"And you want them to know you're normal. Huh? You're just like them." He had rounded on me, and pressed me right against the knife rack. I was holding two glasses of water, one for me and one for him, but I hadn't gotten the chance to offer it to him. "You look like you've been living pretty rough recently."

"Oh yeah. I really need to go out and buy some new mirrors. For some reason I don't seem to have any around the apartment anymore."

There was an agonizing silence, and then Rimbaud snatched the glass from my hand. He took a swig of water, and then patted me on the shoulder. "Hey buddy, sorry if I scared you. I actually didn't even want to talk to you. I hear you've got yourself a roommate. So they say…"

"That's right, we're good friends actually. What else did people say about him?"

"No one seems to have seen him. Ever. Where is he now?"

"Oh, I just made him up to cover my tracks." There was a long and ugly pause. "Sorry, that was a poor joke. Actually you'll never believe this, but he's out at the moment. Huh, first time he's been out by himself for ages. Damn shame for me, I can tell you, because you could be talking to him right now instead of me." A thought, a really nasty thought, was starting to form at the back of my mind.

"What's his name?" Rimbaud asked.

"His name?" I repeated, the thought bubbling away in my mind.

"Yes …" Rimbaud nodded, looking rather tired.

"Daniel," I blurted.

"Same name as yours, huh," he said as he moved to the door. "What a coincidence."

And you see, as I closed the door on Inspector Rimbaud, I realized … *I had never found out my roommate's name.*

I was very nervous indeed when he walked through the door that night. "What's the matter, Daniel?" he asked me. "You're not letting those neighbours get to you, are you? They're just good-for-nothing busybodies!"

"How did you know Serena Gulbis's name?" I asked.

"What? The missing person from all those months ago?" He laughed, and I noticed it was a really nice resonant laugh. "I told you, I saw her on the poster."

"No, but I never said her name when I told you about her being crummy to me in the mail room. So how did you know it was her?"

"You know what I think, Daniel? I think something bad happened today."

"A policeman came round. Asking about those missing people." I swallowed, and actually collapsed against the wall because I couldn't stand up. "Maybe I'm going crazy."

"There is nothing more to worry about, Daniel."

"What are you talking about? I don't know your name, man. For some reason I told Rimbaud you were called 'Daniel.'"

"I do have a name," he said wryly, passing me an uncorked bottle of wine. "And it isn't Daniel."

I swigged the wine down liberally, from the bottle. He declined when I offered it back to him. "But what about these missing people—"

"Oh, they're not going to be a problem anymore. The whole thing is over."

I breathed a sigh of relief. I had a hefty swig of the wine to celebrate. "They caught the guy?"

"Well, the guy achieved what he wanted. Nearly. Just one more to go."

And that's when I realized he was right next to me.

I finished my account and looked around the room, squinting to see where my interrogator was sitting, but I saw nothing. My eyes still hadn't adjusted to the murky blackness. There wasn't even one of those cheap lamps on the desk.

"So that's the story. My roommate, whose name I never found out, wanted to kill me last for some reason! I mean, why would a serial killer kill me last? I was the most likely person to go to the police for all those weeks! Except that no one had seen him and thought I was guilty. Well, thinks I'm guilty."

"Do they really?"

"Oh, don't play coy! I mean, you arrested me, didn't you? Here I am."

"So that's how you remember it."

"Well, funnily enough I *don't* remember it. That was very literally the last thing I remember, and then I was here. Maybe I did make up that roommate. Maybe I am a murderer." I put my head in my hands. "I do feel a bit crazy sometimes."

"Daniel, you're no murderer. You wouldn't hurt a fly." He leaned towards me, and then I saw his face.

It was my roommate! How did he get here? And why, in spite of everything I knew about him, did I immediately feel safe and secure now that he was here? I mean, here I was looking at him, and I smiled in relief!

He rested his hand on my shoulder and squeezed it reassuringly. "The good news is … it worked, Daniel. You got in. Well, I got you in, because I liked you. But let's not tell … the big guy, eh?"

"Who's the big guy? Where have you gotten me in?" I asked.

"Oh Daniel! You may not know it yet, but I think you're going to have real fun here." He clapped his hand on my shoulder and led me out of the room.

It was at that moment that I noticed how very warm the room was. There was only one window, and through it I saw the darkest and highest mountains I had ever seen in my life.

ABOUT THE AUTHORS

SARAH PARRY is a 25 year old New Zealander who has enjoyed reading horror since she was introduced to Edgar Alan Poe's *The Raven* one dark and stormy night. She is currently studying towards her Masters of Teaching in Wellington, where she lives with her sister in a small flat which has been known to make strange noises in the middle of the night.

CRAIG CHARLESWORTH is a qualified nurse who lives and works as a prescriptions administrator in York with his wife Helen and son Emmett. After writing purely for fun for several years he self-released his first novel, *Wolfshead*, in 2012 and his second, *The Cuckoo in Winter*, in 2014. Both are currently available on Amazon. His third novel, *Prince with a Thousand Enemies*, is due sometime in 2017 if he can finally work up the energy to get it finished. An avid *Doctor Who* fan for almost 30 years, he has previously had a short story – The Eternalist – published by Pencil Tip Publishing in the collection *The Temporal Logbook* as well as penning four stories (*Laplace's Demon, Aurum Et Plumbum, A Christmas Story and The Night Before Christmas*) for the *Doctor Who Project* website.

JODIE VAN DE WETERING is a hyperactive word wrangler based in Rockhampton, Australia. At any given moment she might be writing, working in journalism or marketing, doing stand up comedy, or trying to muster the shambolic assortment of artists, wise guys and anarchists that haunt the open mic she runs. They started in a vegetarian restaurant, and these days are based in a mysterious warehouse bar with no official street address. Jodie was first published by *The Doctor Who Project* in her teens, for which she is forever grateful. Since then she's written for the Australian Broadcasting Corporation, literary journals including *Idiom 23* and *Crab Fat*, plenty more for *TDWP* and related projects, and on the backs of a great many envelopes. Concurrent with the release of *Grave Warnings* she has a piece of short fiction included in *Sproutlings*, an Australian anthology of creepy tales themed around wicked plants.

Visit Jodie's website at: www.jodievdw.com

HANNAH G. PARRY has recently completed her PhD in English Literature at Victoria University of Wellington in New Zealand. Her fiction has been published in *The Temporal Logbook* and, as H.G. Parry, in *Daily Science Fiction* and *Intergalactic Medicine Show*. She currently lives with her sister in a flat in Wellington, where there are plenty of stories, but few ghosts.

HAMISH CRAWFORD is the author of the Sherlock Holmes pastiche novel *The Best and Wisest Man* and the short story collection *A Madhouse, Only With More Elegant Jackets*, and several unproduced screenplays, and has contributed stories to *The Temporal Logbook* and *The Doctor Who Project*. He hopes to unveil a second short story collection in 2017 and a young adult novel later that year. He's worried true horror fans may laugh him at because he actually found *Vampire's Kiss* scary when he saw it as a child.

ABOUT THE EDITORS

ROBERT MAMMONE has been writing since he was in high school. His first professional story was sold to *Doctor Who Magazine*. Since then, he has contributed short horror fiction to places like *British Fantasy Society*, The Doctor Who Project, Pseudopod.org, Midnight Echo, *April Moon Books, Dark Minds Press*, Winter Shivers, *The Big Book of Best Short Horror* to name but a few. In recent years he took up the role of editor of *The Doctor Who Project* range and also co-edited Pencil Tip's first *Doctor Who* short story collection, *The Temporal Logbook*.

BOB FURNELL first began to write in elementary school but it wasn't until around 1981, and his discovery of the British television series *Doctor Who* that he started to take writing seriously. He first began contributing to numerous science fiction and television related fan magazines. Over the years he has contributed to such titles as: *Radio Tellyscope, Enlightenment, Jigsaw, Metamorph, ESF, DWB, Andersonic, Star One, Dreamstones, Tellyvision* and numerous others. Since 1999 he has been the Range Editor and Publisher of the longest running *Doctor Who* fiction series *The Doctor Who Project*. He is also the Editor and Publisher of the online e-zine *Whotopia*. His essay on "*Robot*" was featured in *You and Who: Contact Has Been Made: Volume 1* published by Watching Books. Bob founded Pencil Tip Publishing in 2015 and to date has overseen the publication of *The Temporal Logbook* and *The Sapphire and Steel Omnibus*; 2017 will see the publication of *The Temporal Logbook II*. Bob is currently working on developing an original fiction series about the exploits of a 1920s gentleman adventurer.

JEZ STRICKLEY lives in Italy, where he has been teaching for more than ten years. Born on the Isle of Wight, Jez flies back to the UK whenever time permits, and knows his way around Britain's economy-airline hub, otherwise known as Stansted Airport, far too well. Writing came late for Jez, and it wasn't until he was no longer an energetic twenty-something that fan publications came into focus. Since 2008 he has been a contributing editor for the *Doctor Who* e-zine, *Whotopia* and has been a series consultant for *The Doctor Who Project* for longer than he can remember. Along with Rob Mammone and Bob Furnell he co-edited the first volume of the fan anthology *The Temporal Logbook*. Most recently Jez worked as an editor alongside Bob Furnell on the *Sapphire and Steel Omnibus*.

Special Thanks
to the following individuals who gave assistance
in the publication of this book

Jack Drewell
Robert Carpenter
John G. Swogger
Meg MacDonald

THE TEMPORAL LOGBOOK

Twelve Doctors
Twelve windows onto the universe. And the Doctor's life is the history of the universe...

The TEMPORAL LOGBOOK is the telling of that history. From the myths of Ancient Greece to the depths of unknown space, from the life of Lewis Carroll to the horrors of the Black Death, as told by a selection of Doctor Who fandom's best writers.

Available to purchase Lulu.com

All proceeds from this publication will be donated in support of the Positive Living Society of British Columbia which is dedicated to empowering persons living with HIV/AIDS through mutual support and collective action.